HOW I LEARNED FRENCH

Or Certain Events in the Life of

OTTO PULASKI

w w goss

Copyright © 2022 wwgoss

All rights reserved.

ISBN: 979-8-9869215-4-9

Disclaimer
How I Learned French is a fictional tale loosely based on and inspired by true events. Names and characters presented in the work are products of the author's imagination.

wwgoss.com

For my mother,
Emily "Blondie" Goss, née Krasny

Preface

Typically, a preface is not found in a work of fiction. There are notable exceptions, e.g. *The Adventures of Huckleberry Finn*. To justify its inclusion, the preface in a fiction work often serves a specific purpose. Such is the case with *How I Learned French*. That purpose is to ask the reader to not confuse our protagonist, Otto Pulaski, with me, the author. We are, all of us, surrounded by others—fascinating, crazy, lovable, and intelligent others. The extraordinary events in their lives, not mine, are the juicy stuff, the gold. *How I Learned French* personalizes and transforms a selection of these events into events in the life of one Otto Pulaski, events which he, though an imperfect and flawed character, is delighted to share with you.

Bienvenue! / bjɛ̃v.ny / salutation / Welcome!

Introduction

Two things old people do that I try *not* to do is tell stories and complain about health. I was a jock so I don't bitch much when the body hurts. Learning how to shut up is not so easy. We septuagenarians can talk to fucking walls.

All humans tell stories. It's in our DNA. Some stories are better than others, like the *The Odyssey* or *Love's Labour's Lost*. And true raconteurs have TALENT—or at least, so says Donna Leon. Most people, most writers, don't. I'm middling, maybe a C+. I have *talent*, not TALENT. But I have something that's just as important: A story that has to be told, a story that if I didn't scribble it down would earn me a special place in hell; a story that if you didn't listen to it, then, well, you would miss out on something special.

The tales herein for your pleasure and entertainment are ones that I felt compelled to write, a necessity as it were, to fill a hole inside, an empty discontent with the past that craved words. And if those words are fiction as much or more than fact, then so be it. I've set them free to shape a path to understanding something deeper.

We edit memory. Making light of dark times and the reverse. We are happy with ourselves one moment and then condemn that same person the next. We affirm joy, and occasionally we discover a truth or two about ourselves, our dear ones, and the uncaring world. In our hearts, we know well that a great deal of what we say and think is guided by self-serving habit and emotional necessity. Such is the landscape of human memory.

My attempt to unravel the past is disorderly. This story is no memoir. Rather, it's a pseudo-chronology wherein a unifying thread weaves through the pages—namely, *How I Learned French*. I have no affection for the language per se. In fact, I prefer German. However, learning French wanders through a sufficient number of events and experiences to justify that compass point. A side effect of that bearing is a modicum of insight about a handful of French writers. These asides are not intended as lit-crit take-aways, so please don't get wound up in academic froufrou.

How does one not bore oneself with oneself? Apparently, my way of avoiding the tedium is to make my stories juicy. Often, French and sex intersect. Not always, but enough to make it worth warning in advance. And then there are passages sans any mention of either French or sex.

Our breezy romp flits between serious and silly. Perhaps you'll be grateful for these vicissitudes. Or annoyed. For me they were simply part of the path from point A to point B.

Welcome. Enjoy.

Otto Pulaski

Fête: / fȁt / noun / feast, holiday

Zoom 1

I never met my grandparents and for reasons I shall never know or understand my parents rarely spoke of them. On my mother's side, grandmother and grandfather Hoha had been swept up in the wave of post-war depression immigrants from Central Europe and deposited on the West Side of Chicago. They raised six children and lived near the site of the St. Valentine's Day massacre.

My grandfather's side, the Pulaskis, who claimed to be Yankee stock through and through, had less history. The rumor is that in his teens my father stole the family car, drove it from Waterbury, Connecticut, to Chicago, and never spoke to his family again. Somewhere along the way he wrecked the car. That can't be entirely true. At any rate, I can't imagine him having the hutzpah for it. I vaguely remember a conversation he'd had with his twin sister. Until that conversation, I didn't know he had a sister. It was a few days before she passed. I am not naturally curious or I would have pressed my father for more. Soon after, the dirt covered her casket and the memory of her had dimmed. I fact-checked the Mayflower's passenger list for the name "Pulaski." No luck.

I would have dug deeper but some inbred reticence in our family discouraged such inquiries. I learned only recently that my father was not my biological father. So, we had lived a lie. The whole family had lived a lie. Nothing on my birth certificate suggested that he wasn't my biological father. But remember, this was old Chicago. The paperwork was, well, just that. Paper. As an example, when my father was too old to drive—that is, he couldn't see worth beans and couldn't possibly pass a driver's test—the cops stopped by our café, got a slice of pie, and personally handed him a fresh-off-the-press driver's license. The head of the local mafia—back then we called it the syndicate—ate lunch in my dad's café several times a week. You need a driver's license, Harold? No problem. You need a birth certificate? You got it.

And surprise surprise? We're still living the lie and keeping secrets. That's why the only time Papa Otto—that's me—sees his family or talks to them is Thanksgiving. Usually the family talks. They let me listen. It's the big, yearly familial treat from my daughter and the rest of the pack for the persona non grata grandfather. I'm especially not supposed to talk to granddaughter Zadie. She's been coached from an early age to ask no questions. We talk once a year as if from opposite sides of a wall. But the wall is breaking down. The wrecking ball is Zadie.

She's a pain-in-the-ass and wicked smart. Like one Thanksgiving a few years back, out of the blue, she announced that she had become a Jew. I asked her how she, a thirteen-year-old and part of a family that to the best of my knowledge was about as religious as a clam, could be a devout anything. Apparently, she had announced the revelation at breakfast while everyone—including Zadie—was chowing down bacon and eggs. After some discussion she admitted that the real reason was that she liked the sound of Hebrew, her langue du jour. She produced and read something in Hebrew from a dual language book of quotes. I didn't understand a word. Then she read the English, "For the unlearned, old age is winter; for the learned it is the season of the harvest." I'm the oldest and got the message. Like I said, she's wicked smart.

The following year, the big surprise was about hockey. Since we talked only once a year, this stuff hits me rat-a-tat-tat. The hockey shocker was that it wasn't girls' field hockey, but Bobby Orr puck-in-your-teeth hockey. It's about gender identification she says quite matter-of-factly, lecturing like she's got a PhD in Gender and Sexuality. She's started using the boys' bathrooms and threatened to sue her preppy private school if they challenged her. I can kinda of see her pissing at the urinal. Oy! I know that's Yiddish; is it Hebrew, too? The girl's on a collision course with happiness. And that's something I worry about. Just because I don't see Zadie much, doesn't mean I don't worry shitloads about her.

To her credit she doesn't think of herself as special or different. Not a molecule of arrogance, despite perfect SAT scores and having taught herself the nuts and bolts of Hebrew and ancient Greek. I'm still a little miffed that she memorized the first twenty-one lines of The Odyssey *in a day. Took me a month. The girl has grit. The old Greek takes grit. I don't have grit, not anymore. And I'm not particularly smart, either. The little shit—I love her, don't get me wrong—has a punishing intellect.*

It's Thanksgiving, the first Thanksgiving in years that I have NOT physically been with Zadie and family and on the clock. Normally, I was to arrive for brunch and be out the back door by eight p.m., before everybody gets drunk and mean and I maybe drink too much and talk too much about all the things I'm not allowed to talk about around the family—taboo topics like guns, sex, and politics.

I remember last year, when Zadie ambushed me at the dinner table, my granddaughter broke the rule and asked me something she shouldn't have.

"Papa Otto, how did you learn French?"

Now that seems like an innocent enough question. It isn't. Not for me. Asking that question is like cracking the lid on Pandora's box. French is the grease that let's those taboo topics squiggle out of the dark. The adults know this. Zadie doesn't have a clue.

This year, she can't pull me aside and question me in person, not about French or anything else about my sketchy history. COVID has us isolated, spending Thanksgiving alone or within "quarantine pods," sequestered in lonely houses, staring at tiny talking heads on computer screens, interacting with a pixilated version of family. The family—including my daughter and her partner and my granddaughter—takes up a half-dozen or so squares, some of which have one person, some of which have four or five participants weaving in and out of the camera.

Some of the family doesn't want to give up the real estate on Zoom for Zadie to dominate the holiday conversation. Plus, her mom's got a heavy finger on the mute button. Net result: Zadie gets cut short; me too.

We're in different cities and time zones. I'm in Portland, Oregon; Zadie's in Portland, Maine. The rest of the family is in Colorado. Zadie's boarding school, the Penobscot Academy, is a sanitized bubble of wealth and privilege. I forget, but I think it's maybe her third year.

I moved to Portland fifteen years ago, after the city had reached its zenith of coolness. It's since gone downhill. Coincidentally, that was same year Vera Katz left city government. And well after Bud Clark made national news by exposing himself to art! Without a strong and visionary leader, government by commission had proven to be a dysfunctional system. I learned that the "City that Works" was quite the opposite. Leaders were empty-headed, spineless bureaucrats. Citizens were taxed to death and kids had to go to private schools to get a decent education. Trash and the homeless—it's fashionable to call them houseless—were and are ubiquitous. In some ways it's liberating. I mean, I used to recycle, but hell, why not just wing the bottle out the car window. We did that in old Mexico. There are so many goddamned potholes in Portland streets that I can't drive and drink anymore.

At least I'm not living on the street. I feel for those people. I could be there in a heartbeat. The VA and Social Security cover medical and rent. I liked my tiny place in Goose Hollow, with its old-school iron radiators that talked to me and radiated warmth. I heard Zadie's Portland was no Eden either. Unfriendly in an uppity New England way. A poverty of soul. You're old money or you're a dead lobster. At least my Portland has a soul.

I had been carving turkey last year when Zadie hit me with the French business. She had heard rumors. Or I might have let it slip after a couple vodkas. It's unnatural for her to ask questions without making it look like an interrogation.

"Papa Otto," Zadie repeated, "why won't you talk to me about how you learned French?"

My grandchild called me Papa Otto. Kali, my daughter, called me just plain Otto, never father or dad. Sometimes it's "Pops," when she wants my attention. My ex called me all kinds of things; subtle, public humiliation was her specialty. Did she mean to be so mean? Who knows. Regardless, after twenty years of marriage, the yellow brick road had reached a dead end. Elaine unilaterally deemed me sufficiently miserable to warrant divorce. I concurred; the divorce was well-deserved and uncontested.

But back to my story, ma petite histoire, as Casanova would have said.

"I'd love to tell you . . ."

The table went silent, as if I were about to drop trou. Forks and knives stopped clickety-clacking.

". . . later, when you're older," said I.

Everyone started speaking at once, making a team effort to distract Zadie. I could hear the thinking: God help us if that old coot starts saying things.

"Zadie, have you made new friends at school?"

"Otto, how was your flight?"

I had driven. But then no one had asked, and I don't volunteer squat. That's my side of the deal.

"Can you believe them wildfires!"

"Damned hippies smoking dope in the woods what started 'em."

"Got that right . . ."

"Let's ski tomorrow . . ."

The skiing comment wasn't addressed to me, but it got my attention. I had been a biathlete and competed for years.

And so did this comment—get my attention—from Earl, my daughter's recent beau. He leaned toward my granddaughter, pointing a fork at her: "How come you got that boy's haircut, girl?"

I had defended Zadie, resisting the urge to leap over the table and slap Earl on his shiny bald head. "We jealous, Earl? Get a fucking toupee."

He had grunted something to himself and shoved food in his mouth. We never returned to Zadie's question. But that had been last Thanksgiving.

The protocol this year was different with COVID-19, though the family dynamic was unchanged.

"Should I get vaccinated?"

"You know, I'd wait," says Earl from his and Kali's tiny box on the screen. Yes, by some miracle Earl is still in the picture. "Needs more research," he authoritatively proclaims. Earl's a contractor, builds big office and condo buildings, so he ought to know. He's a professional everything.

"Your body is a temple's what my Pilates teacher says . . ." Someone else says.

As far as vaccination went, half of these idiots, the half from my daughter's new salt-of-the-earth hubby's family, knew with the certainty only the faithful harbor that the vaccines were a CIA conspiracy or Bill Gates nano-bots. They actually debated between these two highly plausible explanations.

Her first hubby, now him I had liked. We got along. But his third tour in Iraq was his last anything. Guy liked to read and shoot, like me. The guy's name was Guy. A real sweetheart, quiet and gentle with children, with everybody really. I never saw him as an Army guy. That's how real Army guys are.

Zadie ignored the vaccination talk and lobbed the French-bomb again.

"I'm older now, Papa Otto. Remember. You said last year, you'd tell me when I was older."

"Tell you what Zadie?" I had forgotten. I'd been snockered last year and was entitled to forget. I was working up to being snockered this year.

"About French, how you learned French?"

I didn't bother to mute.

"Merde. Fuck"

I had self-quarantined like much of the country except for the Looney Toon sycophants following the Looney-Toon-in-Chief. That moniker came from a once colleague of mine who had started his career as a writer at Fortune magazine and eventually co-managed Time's venture capital fund. That had been in the good-old-days when Hank Luce ran the show and Time Inc. could invest in anything it damned-well pleased. Back then, he told me, the reporters would draw straws and the short straw got stuck having lunch with Looney Toon when

Looney Toon needed publicity; the man had blathered about himself ad nauseam and never made sense. Some things never change.

"Otto! Zadie's mother's head popped sideways into a tile on the screen. Back home in Aspen, she was cooking, mostly off camera. Her chin was dabbed with flour.

"You're swearing . . ."

"Oh, crap," I said.

"Much better!" She smiled. Her smile made a vertical emoji-esque squiggle on the screen and her hair was sideways, like she was calling from the International Space Station.

"Mom, I think Papa Otto is cute when he swears."

They had the same smiles, reminding me how much I loved them both.

"There's chocolate on your chin," I pointed to my own chin to show her where. "And your head's sideways."

Kali is a good cook. Elaine, too. I may not have served as a moral compass, but I did teach them how to grow starter and make Tartine-worthy country bread, bread with great crumb and a hearty crust.

"I'm making a cake in honor of Zadie. Flourless chocolate—the kind you and Mom used to make for me. Even if she's not here," my daughter said. Zadie's birthday was on the twenty-sixth. This year it fell on Thanksgiving day. "I mean, Zadie's not here. Where is Mom, Otto? She was in the south of France, a watercolor workshop, but after . . ."

"Elaine is . . . I don't know."

And I wouldn't. My ex and I don't talk much. Odd that Kali even asked. Elaine and I last spoke when her dog died. She loves dogs.

She's been through a lot of them. Good at putting them down when it's time. She never quite got that option with me but I'm sure she would have rallied. Selfless love drives her. I couldn't do it; I'm selfish.

Zadie says that Kali says that Elaine says that it's still too painful to see me. Maybe. It could also be the case that what pains her is that I'm so annoying. My ex has multiple houses, like the rich do so they always have something to bitch about. I have to give it to her: her houses are oddly peaceful, even joyful, like her painting.

Zadie brought me back. "Papa Otto . . ."

The dorm room showed in the background. Zadie ignored her mom. She wouldn't have ignored Elaine if she were on the call. Zadie and Elaine had a good relationship, for which I was grateful.

"Just like you," I said, ignoring her mom as well. "Same as you, in high school. But I studied French, not Greek or—"

"Latin!" she added the update before returning to her question. "But that's not what I heard . . ."

It's weird, all these eyes staring at you from the computer screen like one giant bug-eyed bug.

The eyes and mouths froze. At first, I thought it was the computer. But the screen had not frozen; only their expressions. I wanted to shout. "Relax, I'm nothin' but electrons. I'm not going to bite." What are they afraid of?

I kinda get where they're coming from. I'd grown up in town run by the mob. Plus, two close friends of mine had done serious time: one dealt coke and the other, a U.K. currency trader, specialized in tax avoidance schemes. And there was a guy I climbed with who had killed his mother. He got twenty plus. And then, there was mon ami, "Bumper."

Bumper

Bumper had a meth-thin body, facial scars, bug-eyes and buck teeth. He was a well-rounded climber. We climbed together for a year or so. He was also a well-rounded psychopath. He had a black belt in some martial art, had aced the LSAT (but dropped out of law school), and played chess blindfolded. Besides ranting at "the man" and chess and climbing, Bumper loved to hurt people. In his twenties he did a spell as an undercover "vagrant" for the Colorado Springs police force. Bumper would set himself up to be mugged and then beat hapless muggers half to death. His family had moved to the States from Paris when Bumper was six. By the time I met Bumper he had been cast out of the family and didn't remember a word of French. This latter fact Elaine never accepted. She swore that she had heard Bumper and me speaking French.

After I married and settled down, I lost touch with Bumper. Then, one lovely spring evening when the cherry tree on the front lawn blossomed to operatic excess, Bumper showed up at my doorstep. Elaine, Kali, and I were heading out the door for some gala and dressed to the nines. I was in a tux. Bumper had arrived in a rusted-out station wagon with bald tires. He was shirtless and smelly, as were the one-armed driver and the passenger sprawled across the back seat. I told Elaine and Kali to stay put and not call the cops. She was shaking because these guys looked like bad news and they were, projecting visions of *A*

Clockwork Orange. I knew Bumper well enough, and I told her to fucking chill.

It turned out Bumper was drifting and hanging with the one-armed fat guy driving the car. I was introduced to One Arm, who was a hitman for some drug-dealing commune in New Mexico, and then to the skinny shit in the back seat, who looked all of seventeen. He was French and didn't speak *un mot* of English.

French kid's wide black pupils found me. "Des drogues?"

"Non. Désolé," I answered. The eyes saddened and wandered off.

The three of them were sharing swill from a jug of brownish, acid-laced hootch. Bumper said he just wanted to say "hi." It had been while, years, in fact. He looked at Kali and slimy kid in the back seat and smiled, like these two were meant for each other. Always thinking of others, that's my Bumper.

We hugged—me in the tux and him in his smarmy oozing skin. Fat Guy scowled. I asked Bumper if he needed money. He didn't. And they left. See ya in five years.

Elaine was still trembling after they left. "They look like murderers! I'm going to call the police."

"Yup. They are." I said. "And nope, don't call the cops."

Elaine hadn't listened to me. One Arm had found out. I don't know the details, but One Arm wanted revenge. As a favor, Bumper made him go away. Knowing Bumper, he probably cut off the guy's other arm and then rolled One Arm into the Rio Grande.

As a consequence of whatever the hell he did on my behalf, Bumper was on the lam. I helped him resettle in the real

Mexico and I gave him twenty K of Elaine's money. When I left Bumper, he was living in Maguarichic, Chihuahua, a tiny, mining town at the head of a draw that descends into the bowels of the Barrancas del Cobre, el destino más grandioso de México. It's an eight-hour drive along a riverbed to get to Maguarichic. Locals, including neighboring Tarahumara, live in mud-floor houses (very clean, however) and use geothermal water for bathing and steaming fissures for cooking. In a way, Maguarichic was paradise. We sipped tesquino, chewed goat, and soaked in the hot springs. After a couple of weeks helping Bumper settle in, I returned to Colorado. Again, I asked Elaine to not call the authorities. She complied but put new locks on the doors. She never trusted me after the Bumper thing. Nobody in the her family did.

I accept, as a fact of human nature, that we, my fellow man and, I suspect, many of my fellow women, are a murderous lot. Down deep an enduring river of evil and violence flows through our veins and thoughts. In my agro years, like the disaffected Bumper, I begged for an excuse to unleash that violence. He found a voice for his, as did others in my life. My cold affection for violence diminished over the years, but the stigma remained and like an indelible démon it haunted Elaine and by extension her family and my daughter, Kali.

And Bumper? Well, that was then and, who knows, maybe now he's like Mr. Normal. I hope so.

Attends: / a.tã / 2nd pers. sing. pres. ind. of attendre / wait

Zoom 2

My attention returned to the conversation. I punted the "How I learned French" question. "You're still too young."

Zadie contested: "Nope. I'm plenty old enough, Papa Otto."

She was right. She's smart. Zadie had been given the option to flat-out skip high school and go straight to college. That's how smart she is. To the family's credit nobody made a big deal out it. She told me she had decided to stick with high school because otherwise she'd miss out on a lot of fun. And she wanted to have fun while she could. She could study whatever she wanted and play hockey and make friends her own age. Plus, she wouldn't stick out like some kind of freak in college. The world's a dark place. That was a hell of a mature decision.

Zadie and I have this bond. It's from sharing the same foxhole and battling aorist forms in ancient Greek. That bond makes it hard for me to not be straight with her.

When I was her age, I was a superlative liar. My buddies called me "the silver tongue." No more. Now I suck at lying. I try but my heart's not in it and the lies never come out quite the way I expect. And the memory is slipping, for almost everything. The exception is if there's a real emotional connection. But the lying about mundane stuff precipitates a dread that the lies will come back and bite me in the ass.

"What else is for dinner, Kali?" I asked.

My daughter, Kali with the chocolate on her chin, was named by my ex, who came up with the name even though she had never studied Greek. Or maybe she named Kali after the badass Hindu goddess, Kali, the destroyer of evil forces. There's evil in every family. You gotta keep a lid on it.

"Corn soufflé."

"You helping, Zadie?" It was one of her favorite dishes.

"Papa Otto, I'm in Maine—duh."

"Yeah, I forget. See, I forget shit."

"When convenient, Papa Otto," Zadie parried.

Mom played peacemaker. "Don't be rude, sweetie."

I played another distraction card. "How's school going?"

I got the lame response the lame question deserved. "Fine."

"Not fine," Kali butted in. "She was bullied. I spoke to the headmaster."

"I didn't want you to do that, Mom," Zadie didn't want that conversation to have happened nor this one. "Do we have to talk about this?"

"About the haircut?" I asked, meaning, of course, her drift toward trans.

"Yeah, Zadie confirmed, "the hair."

There had to have been more to the story. I gave her an easy out and she took it.

"Next time, Zadie, kick 'em in the nuts or tits or whatever."

The comment silenced bobblehead chatter in the background.

"You might lose a fight," I said, "but you'll win the war. Trust me."

I meant what I said. Self-respect didn't come from a worried mother's conversation with a headmaster. It came from standing up for yourself. Why not? You're gonna hurt either way, better to get it over with when you young and heal fast.

"Well, Papa Otto?" Zadie spoke to a mostly silent audience.

"Okay," I said, knowing fully the following: First, Zadie's trans issue was not an appropriate topic for the family forum. And second, I wasn't going to be let off the hook this year. My answer, the truth, was quite straightforward. "My first exposure to French was before high school. I was a little younger than you and I thought I was going to die."

"Die for real?"

"For real, yes." I paused for dramatic effect. "I was climbing at Devil's Lake, Wisconsin, and I got stuck on a cliff. This old French guy saved my ass. We became friends."

Jean DeLambert

In the 1950s, hot-wiring a car was a piece of cake. The wires leading to the battery, ignition, and starter were either under the steering wheel column or the ignition key. You just unplug them or cut them free. There were no alarms and no triggers to disable the starter. The wires are color-coded, so it's smart to have a light to see colors. Twist the ignition wire together with the battery wire. Test the radio to see if you have a connection. Touch the starter wire to the two battery wires just long enough for the car to start. Rev it up and off you go.

The first car I hot-wired was an old, pea-green station wagon. I don't remember the make or model. We needed a station wagon because my buddies and I had decided to go camping at Devil's Lake, Wisconsin—about a three-hour drive from Chicago. We scrounged together makeshift camping gear and packed a cooler with cookies, milk, cokes and bologna and mayo sandwiches on Wonder Bread. On departure day there was only one problem. We didn't have a car.

Among the four of us, Vlacek and Svoboda were the oldest and had drivers' licenses. Each thought the other had lined up a car. That night, we met in Vlacek's garage where we assembled our gear and strategized. Being the youngest and smallest of the four of us, I couldn't drive. I had, however, masterminded a chain of lies for our respective parents. Young silver-tongue smoothly explained to my parents and my friends' parents exactly who was staying with whom. The shell game worked. Two of us, Svoboda and me, were decent students; our parents foolishly trusted us. As long as the respective parents didn't compare notes, an unlikely event because they either didn't know or didn't like each other, we'd be okay. Back then parents didn't hover. And back then parents had no problem whacking a kid across the head if he or she screwed up. I've always been on the fence about cuffing the kids. Didn't do it much, more out of peer pressure than any conviction that it was wrong.

We had lifted a couple of cars before. The normal drill was, we'd drive it for an hour and park it someplace funny like the middle of a railroad track (okay, that's not so funny now) or set up a ramp and leave it in the middle of a fountain. The camping escapade took our pilfering to a new level, that of a complex and extended adventure. We figured since we were in Illinois all we had to do was cross the border to Wisconsin and we'd be off of the radar of the Illinois State Troopers. We'd lift the car and cross the border before anyone noticed the missing vehicle. That was the theory from the straight-A-students. At the end of the camping adventure, we'd steal a Wisconsin license plate, slap it on our cruiser near the border and drive home.

Our flawless plan almost worked. Dawn broke as we crossed into Wisconsin. We cranked up the tunes. Our driver was pounding out the beat on the steering wheel and stomping his feet. At least we weren't drinking. The station wagon swayed with the beat, and we swerved into a hard-edged pothole on the side of the road. The tire blew, I literally bit my tongue, and the radio died. I was sleeping in the back but the bump and blowout woke me. We coasted to a stop on the grassy embankment beside the pavement. Wisps of smoke came up from under the dash. The wires looked like particolored hash browns.

This was dairy country, hilly and pastoral and no town in sight. A bunch of cows eyeballed us with their billiard-ball-sized eyeballs. They chewed and stared, unthinking, like it was the hundredth time they had seen four teenage kids in a hot-wired car with a shitload of camping gear.

"Whadda we do?" asked Vlacek, the biggest of us, our driver and not a straight-A-student.

They looked at me because I always had a plan. That was my other role, other than the silver tongue gig. I was awake now, silver tongue oozing little blood but swollen.

"Okay. We can't steal another car. Agreed?" The swelling made the 't' a 'th.'

We looked around and saw a farmhouse a quarter mile off. There were a couple of trucks parked beside an adjoining barn but it would be impossible to take one without being noticed. We didn't have the brave to approach the people who lived there. I was smooth but not that good.

"So we're screwed," Vlacek's voice warbled. Definitely not his usual big-tough-guy tone.

"Gonna have to hitchhike or walk from here," I stated the obvious. "Man, did we bring shitloads of crap."

Svoboda stared at the gear stuffed in the back of the car and then looked at me, "Yeah, guess so."

This time, we all turned our heads and stared with him. We couldn't abandon our stuff with the car and we had no idea where we were. Nobody had paid attention to the map after we'd crossed the border.

"That's my uncle's cooler," one of them said.

"We'll bury it," Svoboda said. I knew where he was going.

"And," I added, "the sleeping bags and the stove . . . everything we can't carry, we bury. We hitch to town, take the bus home. Maybe your sister can drive us back next weekend and we'll dig the stuff up."

Nobody had a better plan, and the sun was raising the shade for a new day. We schlepped everything we couldn't credibly carry on our person a quarter mile up a hill to a cluster of bushes. We buried some of the gear and camouflaged the rest with dirt and branches. It was a brutal and nervous hour of work. Not a single vehicle drove by. Farmers must have been milking cows. Our final act was to roll the car safely off the road. We learned that rolling a car with a flat tire was a bitch.

We found a card in the glove box. *Jeffrey Williams, Aetna Insurance.* Vlacek put the card under the windshield wiper saying the State Patrol would think Williams had just abandoned his car after the flat. I removed it. As soon as the police found the vehicle, they'd run a search and find out who the owner was. It would still take time for the search and time to contact Williams and determine if he was the owner. Not knowing the bus schedule or even where the closest town was, we needed as much time as we could get.

We walked along the road for five minutes and miraculously got a ride in the back of a passing truck to a town I don't remember the name of. As luck would have it, a bus was leaving for Chicago that morning within the hour. We paid cash and made an expeditious getaway. A week later, Vlacek and his sister retrieved everything without a hitch.

Word got around. Not from me, but because the story was too good to stay quiet for long.

One day, a month or so later, a muscled guy in his thirties walked into my parents café looking for me. I was washing dishes and watched him talk with my mom at the cash register. He approached me and put his hand on my shoulder. I was up to my elbows in a sink of sudsy water. I was afraid he was going to dunk my head in the sink basin.

"Otto," he addressed me. "You know who I am?"

I did. He was the school counselor. There were almost five thousand students in my high school and only a couple of "counselors." You disrespected a counselor at your peril.

"Yes, sir."

"I hear you like camping."

"Yes, sir."

"Well, you're going camping next week."

"But it's school—"

"Not for you, Otto. You're suspended, son. Do camp; behave, and you come back to school the week after. You *do* like camping?"

"Yes, sir. I sure do." He knew what we had done.

I kept looking at Mom. She was talking to my dad who was fingering his belt. I was in for it.

"Monday, eight sharp. You know what to pack. Leave the shiv. Got that?"

I raised my eyebrows, *huh*? He didn't respond.

"A bus from school will pick you up."

Leave the shiv? Good grief. If I had to do in somebody, why would I use a knife? Dad had a loaded .38 in the top drawer of the bureau by the front door and another one in the glove box of the Pontiac—that's a car, by the way. The gun in the glove box was a silver-plated revolver, even the handle was silver-plated. I worried when we'd hit a bump and the damn thing banged around in there, like it wanted out to express its telos and shoot someone, anyone, purely out of philosophical necessity. Sometimes I'd just stare at the glovebox. Dad made weekly drives to the bank. Once in a while we'd stop at this creepy bar that was always closed. He'd drop off cash with a weird friend of his that I never met. I saw the friend a few times, at the door. The friend was big, three-or-four hundred pounds big. His name was Hank. Dad said Hank was a communist and liked classical music.

Pick-up day came. The promised van arrived to take me to the promised camp. I hopped aboard with a small pack and a paper bag with a sandwich mom gave me. They had sleeping bags and cooking stuff for us.

When the driver announced that we were going to Devil's Lake, I figured I was hearing things and asked him to repeat what he had said. He yelled for the dozen punks in the van to shut up.

I'm sure I was the only one in the bus who had a clue where Devil's Lake was. This was crazy. I had been caught stealing candy and for punishment, they were sending me back to the candy store!

The other crazy thing was that there were a couple black boys in the group. My school and pretty much all of Cicero were whiter than white—Wops, Polacks, Bohunks, even Russkies. No Blacks and no Spics. Cicero Avenue was our Berlin Wall, our Maginot Line. The west side was white, the east side black. After ten p.m. nobody crossed that street. I mean, you could, but only if you were looking for trouble. The black kids must have come from a school on the wrong side. I didn't care, but a lot of folks in Cicero would shit a brick if they knew I was going camping with a couple of blacks.

I assessed this pack of Hoods-in-the-Woods wards as juvenile delinquents-light. None of these punks were the truly tough, not like the big Italians who, because of their size and heritage, interned with the local mafia and guys who had done time. I knew those youths. They came to our café with the boss. When these interns were young and poor, my parents had supported them. My folks fed any kid in our hood who needed a meal. They did that for years and never asked for a nickel. What this meant was that no one messed with me. A black guy worked at our joint, a friend of my dad's. He worked mornings at the café, and nobody messed with him. That's how inviolable we were. The wannabe toughies in this van were a bunch of losers and the twenty-something, do-gooder group leader was going to be one of those types who tries and fails to find that middle ground between being your best bud and an asshole.

(God, I was such an arrogant, little prick.)

After a couple of days of nature walks and military calisthenics, we got our first real look at the Lake. The big event was a canoe excursion, and everybody was assigned a canoe, instructions to follow. I needed a break and begged off on grounds that I couldn't swim and nobody in our group was qualified to rescue me if I went overboard. I guessed that that would be the case. The truth was, I had been on the swim team, swam like a fish, and had even been through lifeguard training. But junior counselor didn't know that and let me stay at the campsite with strict instructions to not "wander off." Last minute, he almost canceled the boating adventure and had an out-loud conversation with himself about the weather. It was overcast. I told him I was going to be fine. Then he repeated my words back to me. Do-gooder had no brain of his own. A guy that easy to convince shouldn't be in charge of a bunch of punks.

A confused organizational effort preceded the fleet paddling off. When they disappeared around a small peninsula it was like somebody threw open the door and on the other side the day was writ large. An endless expanse awaited. The time to wander off had come.

Other than the lake itself, the most intriguing feature of Devil's Lake was the columnated band of pink and purple quartzite cliffs along the East Bank Trail. That's where I headed.

Up was always important to me. It was how I saved my skinny ass in Cicero when bad guys or cops chased me. I'd vanish down a dark alley and climb a fence or side of a garage to rooftop safety. I was good at it and over time had dialed in a half-dozen escape routes. I could do them with my eyes closed. I was fearless and I was fast.

The quartzite columns poked out of a talus field of lichen-covered rock jeweled with dew. At the bottom of one particular rock formation, a group from the Chicago Mountaineering Club milled around. I found a rock to sit on and watched as pairs of climbers roped up and made their way up routes with funny names. The routes didn't look hard, not compared to the parkour I was used to. I sauntered up to an arête, wiped mud off my sneakers and onto my pants and started up—free soloing. A small crowd gathered below to watch. I'm sure they expected me to stop after I was a couple feet off the ground, but I didn't. Cicero was an industrial city. I'd climbed factory walls four or five stories high.

About thirty feet up, a couple of folks started shouting. One said, "Get help, hurry."

I got stuck ten feet from the top. But I wasn't alone. A quiet man in his late fifties was beside me, maybe eight feet away; he had mostly finished leading the route he had been climbing. He clipped into a piton and tied himself off, leaving a loop of slack so he could maneuver. Smiling when our gaze connected, he took off his baseball hat and wiped his brow with it. He was mostly bald and moved with deliberation.

"You zee. . ." Using a calm voice, he showed me the rope in his hand. "With zees corde d'escalade you climb routes zat are much, much harder. Cela," he pointed to the arête I had been climbing, "eez too e-zee for *you!*" The tone of voice, the lift at the end of the sentence, implied respect. Respect for me.

"Yeah, 'suppose," I said.

I'd expected to be lectured or scolded or screamed at. But this man was doing the opposite. He was encouraging me to try something more challenging.

"Where I am eez much harder. You want to try?"

"Sure," I said. But I was stuck. He knew it and I knew it. The people below couldn't see us well enough to know how precarious and dangerous my position was. The soles of my sneakers were oozing off of the damp footholds. Quartzite is slippery as snot when it's wet.

"Attends!" he said. He repeated the word several times. If I started to move or fidget, he'd say it again and hold his hand in the air, motionless, an indication that I shouldn't move a muscle.

"Attends."

That was my first real word of French. It means *wait*, or *hold on* in English. The context in this case made the meaning clear: *hang on*.

He traversed toward me. The footwork was delicate. He handed me a bight of rope which I wrapped around my waist. He took the bight, made a knot, and then used a carabiner to attach it to another knot he had tied in the rope, effectively tying the two of us together. There was about ten feet of slack.

I could feel the crowd below breathing and watching.

He pointed to himself and then held up one finger and pointed to himself, "J'y vais."

Then he pointed to me and held up two fingers, "Tu vas. Okay?"

I got it. He would go first. I would follow. He returned to his perch and held the rope secure as I stepped across to an improved stance beside him at the piton.

"Nom?"

"Otto," I said.

"Jean DeLambert. . . . plaisir!"

I think DeLambert recognized a fellow spirit in me, a younger version of himself, a boy as brave and curious—and perhaps as foolish—as he had been at that age. He took me under his wing, introduced me to a few other members of the Chicago Mountaineering Club. I became a regular tag-along. Hoods-in-the-Woods had worked. I spent weekends practicing knots, rappelling off buildings, and climbing with real climbers at Devil's Lake and other Midwestern crags. On trips with DeLambert and his family, everyone spoke French. I listened and understood nothing.

Zoom 3

Zadie seemed satisfied by the French-guy-saved-my-ass response. Kali looked relieved, as did others on the call. I'd talked about the climbing but only hinted at stealing the car. Tame stuff compared to the riots, massacres, and protests these days.

Black Lives Matter is a legitimate cause, for sure. Protests had run over a hundred days straight in Portland and cost the city millions in damage. To be fair, much of the damage was NOT by the protesters. The vandalism and senseless destruction came from two groups who used the protests for cover.

The first group was local and well-organized. One or two people would set fires and break windows at locations like Pioneer Square so their buddies could drive up in vans and fill them with stolen goods—Louis Vuitton bags, iPhones, whatever the hell they could carry. They'd break into places that were vulnerable. They tried to burn down a friend of mine's gallery after a failed attempt to force the door open.

The other group of criminals were out-of-town Proud Boys from Vancouver, Washington, and anywhere in Texas but Austin. Incited by their Looney Toon spokespeople, the Texans had driven thousands of miles to swoop down on "lawless" Portland protestors. Nobody-but-nobody wanted these assholes in Portland. Not the genuine protesters, not the police, certainly not the guy on the street, and not the Feds that the Looney Toon-in-Chief had forced on the city.

I'm trying to be a non-violent guy these days. But I gotta admit, the right-wing jerkoffs pushed my buttons and I thought more than once about cleaning my rifles. I'm an okay shot. I would've loved plinking a beer can out of the hands of one of these yahoos parading up and down the Willamette River in his dumb-shit speedboat. Whenever they had these boat parades, one of the boats would end up sinking. Man, they're dumb!

But the Portland reportage is a digression. I've been avoiding something, namely that the car camping caper was only half the story about why Devil's Lake and why "Attends" is burned into my brainbox.

"Papa Otto?"

"Yes, Zadie."

"What else did you do at Devil's Lake? I mean, what did teenagers do then?"

Kali redirected Zadie's question, "Otto, didn't you tell me you learned to dance . . ."

"Yeah. Sort of. I'd never danced before and Devil's Lake had this gazebo-like structure, but enclosed because it was chilly at night. People played music from a jukebox and there was one of those spinning mirror-balls flinging colored specs of light across the floor and ceiling."

"That's so cool!" Zadie found this cool?

"Give me a song. Like a song you danced to!"

"Wah-Watusi, The Monster Mash, Gloria . . ."

"Wait, wait!" I heard her fingers scampering across the keyboard. Moments later the Orlons were belting out the chorus, Wah, wah-a Watusi / C'mon and take a chance and get-a with this dance . . .

We waited and watched in silence as Zadie retrieved The Monster Mash and played a video.

"Can you do that?"

"Hell yeah!"

"Teach me, like next time we're together for real."

"Love to." I'm a fair dancer. Mostly Salsa. Elaine wasn't keen on dancing, but let me out of the house once in a while. I'd taught Kali East Coast Swing.

Next Zadie played Gloria.

"Don't play that one, please," I asked.

"Why not?"

I grimaced. "It hurts, Zadie."

"Oh, was it a girlfriend, Papa Otto? Did you meet a girl at the Gazebo?"

Am I that transparent? Is Zadie psychic? I looked at the collage on my computer screen, hoping for rescue.

"Another time," I said.

"When we shall dance. Promise?"

"Sure," I did my best to not look like I was lying, "I promise."

I had crossed my fingers when I made the promise. I kept them crossed for a while, staring at the middle finger, right hand. The first body part to experience a woman's sex. That's what the French call it, one's sex. The sex reference is universal, men or women, c'est le même.

People talk about teens these days being younger when they experience sex. Between the internet and sex-ed there's little to no mystery to the physical aspect human sexuality anymore. It's a oversimplification but often true that for kids today it's simply a matter of when and with whom, not the limitless morass of ignorance and fear and misinformation of my generation.

G.L.O.R.I.A.

My buddy Vlacek believed that if he didn't keep his penis upright in his underwear twenty-four-seven then the poor thing would flop to the left or to the right and grow to become grotesquely disfigured. He was always reaching down in his pants or rolling up the waist of his undies as tight as possible to hold the little bugger in place. We laughed at him, but he was adamant. "You'll see," he forewarned. "Someday you guys are gonna have these cockeyed dicks and mine is gonna be like an oak." Back then, what did I know? Maybe he was right. I worried about it. And maybe these days he goes tug-tug on that mighty oak and thinks, "What a good boy was I."

Despite our fumbling and ignorance, sex happened. The first rape I heard about was close to home. It happened on the fire escape of my elementary school, in a three-story-tall alcove. I used to climb from the top of the fire escape to get to the roof of the building. Rape, to me, is something dark and dirty in the psyche. The rape happened in an appropriately dark and dirty corner on the ground level, a place where shitheads from junior high would hang out and smoke and where the ground was littered with butts and broken glass. It was during the day, middle of the afternoon. I was in class. Nobody heard a thing. I didn't know the girl, a sixth-grader, or the offender. I just heard the talk the next day when the guards were patrolling the playground and giving everybody the evil eye. Rape was bad, whatever it was. I didn't even know what the word "rape" meant, what it physically entailed or the mental consequences. Like my equally ignorant friends, I pretended I understood. There was no internet and parents were useless. If we mustered the courage to ask a question, the only answer we got was, "Go to church."

Vlacek was Catholic. He hated church, but, who knows, maybe a priest gave him that sage counsel about his dick. Hell, he probably helped with the straight oak business.

Having a 'social experience' was part of the Devil's Lake rehab drill. Bad boys being made to dance. Do-gooder Counselor, like a mother duck, lined us up and led his brood into the gazebo. We groaned but didn't have a choice; dance was part of the program. I was last in line. There were chairs along the walls but not enough for us to sit together. I was walking toward an empty chair when a girl, a little older than me, came up behind me and took my arm. Just like that! It scared the piss out of me.

"Want to dance?"

"What?" I said.

"C'mon."

She was way out of my league. I'm quite sure every girl at that time would have been out of my league. I was no player, and this girl was the most beautiful girl I had ever laid eyes on. I smelled whisky on her breath. I didn't know how to dance, but she showed me and we sweated through one song and then another. Unfamiliar bodies filled the gazebo and Do-gooder lost track of his flock. I saw him milling about the crowd. He ran across the black kids. They stood out because they were black and because they were sorta dancing. The others were drifting around and probably trying to score some weed—you know, something to brag about when they got back to Chicago. One of them, I know, bought a joint of oregano. He got high from it.

Sandy, that was her name, my Helen of the gazebo. She led me out the door and walked me a couple hundred yards along an unlit path to a trailer hitched to an enormous pickup truck, the kind with the double wheels on the rear axle.

"My parents' rig," she announced as she opened the door to the trailer and climbed the steps with me obediently in tow. My eyes adjusted to the darkness, and I saw her pull out a bottle of something from a built-in cupboard. She arched her back against the wall, threw back her head, and took a swig.

"Want some?"

I declined. Then her other hand took mine and placed it on her breast. I so wanted to be cool. I fumbled around and rubbed hard against her. Was that cool? Or is the right thing to just stand at attention and wait. She slid my hand across her belly and unbuttoned her jeans. I gave in, thinking this is what she wanted. My hand dove into that great mystery under her panties. That middle finger, like a hummingbird after nectar, a drone finding its target, a batter connecting with a fastball—how many cheesy metaphors are there to express the fear and excitement as that little finger glided into her vagina. She rubbed against me and I came in my pants to a white flash produced not from the sex but from the lights coming on in the trailer.

"Out!" her mother screamed. "Who the hell do you think you are?"

The mom was drunk. Sandy set the bottle next to me, as if I'd been the one drinking.

"Drink ma liquor, ya little prick?!"

It's one thing to finger-fuck an alcoholic mother's daughter. It's an altogether greater offense is to nip from her stash.

I ducked under her arm, thinking she was going after me but saw it was really the bottle she had been reaching for. I bolted to the door and glimpsed Sandy straightening her jeans and doing something between laughing and crying. About twenty yards from the trailer, I passed the father. He was scary-big, especially in the dark. He watched me jog by but kept walking.

Mind-blowing. If that was sex, well, then sex was mind-blowing. I wanted more.

So back to *Gloria*; what does this have to do with *Gloria*? Before our untimely separation back at the trailer, Sandy had written her number on my hand. She was from Chicago as well and lived in an upscale neighborhood on the North Side. When back in Cicero, I had called her a half-dozen times, but I hung up each time because one of her parents answered. One night, I got lucky.

"Sandy?"

"Yeah, hi. Who's this?"

"Otto."

"Oh. The Baraboo kid?"

Baraboo is the small town close to Devil's Lake. Why would she think I was from there? Was there another Baraboo kid? I hadn't thought about that.

"Can I see you?"

"No. I gotta boyfriend. A musician. He's a singer with a band."

"What band?" I don't know why I asked. I knew nothing about bands or pop music.

"Shadows of Knight."

"Huh."

I waited for her to say something. She waited for me to say something. I didn't know the band but found out later that they were Chicago locals, but a little famous anyway.

"The *Gloria* band. Gotta go. Bye," she said.

"Wait!"

Nothing.

"Attends," I said into the dead phone. I'd whispered the word in a French accent. I had hoped that maybe she was still on the line and that the word would get her attention like it gotten mine up on that cliff.

Was there a click? I couldn't tell.

I should have sussed things out. At the gazebo, she had played *Gloria* on the jukebox, a couple times. When she sang the lyrics—I think she was stoned—she mouthed each letter so you could tell what it was a mile away. My favorite was the "L," when she'd throw her head back and the bottom of her tongue was exposed as the tip licked her top teeth. Her tongue and lips worshipped those letters. Each letter of G-L-O-R-I-A, you see, it was like each letter brought her one step closer to coming. I think she had been saying them when I slid my finger inside her. At least in her head, to herself. She had pushed my hand hard against her sex. She'd hit R when the lights went on. I had thought we were just Sandy and Otto. Idiot.

Would I see her again? Would I ever be with someone like that again?

"Attends . . ."

Ça ira: / sa i.ʁa/ 3rd pers. nom. pronoun + 3rd pers.
sing. future of aller / It will be okay.

Zoom 4

"My French teacher's a stiff," Zadie said.

"I didn't know you were taking French. Still doing Greek and Latin?"

"Dropped Latin. Latin was okay, but had a conflict with Calc. Did you have a lot of homework?" Zadie asked. "You know when you took French in high school? We get super dumped on."

I'm sure that was true. A lot of COVID-era kids got shitloads more homework to make up for the lost class time. A lot more students were simply ignored.

"None in French. Never brought a book home." That was true. In high school I'd almost never brought home a book for anything.

"C'mon—"

"You, c'mon! French is un jeu d'enfant. Child's play." I added that for the non-French speaking listeners. "Only two genders and well-behaved adjectives. Ancient Greek nouns have three genders, a dual in addition to singular and plural, five cases with specialized forms, and fussy adjectival prefixes and suffixes galore!"

I rattled off a few examples of French noun and adjective agreement, then pronoun and verb.

Zadie interrupted and added to the last string, finishing with 'he's happy, she's happy.' " —il est heureux, elle est heureuse. Booorrring, Papa Otto!"

I earned that for drifting into lecture mode. I'd been tutoring here and there. The uppity lecturing tone was a bad habit. I'm not really a nice guy and, as you'll learn, loaded with bad habits.

Kali erupted. "Zadie, be nice!"

"No. And why?" she said. Was the interrogative aimed at Kali or me. Was it why be nice, or why no books?

I assumed books and answered truthfully: "I paid attention in class."

"Uh huh. Like I believe that, Papa Otto."

Now you probably think I'm boasting about remembering French vocabulary, especially after I had confessed to having an indifferent and inferior memory. There was a reason, however. Zadie will figure it out one day when she walks into a class and wets her pants over a brilliant, attractive, young professor reading e. e. cummings' She being Brand. *Or maybe the poem would backfire and offend her take on gender. Nah, that poem would snag anyone, any sex.*

Mlle Lachenal

The door creaked, announcing my tardy arrival to a class in progress. The teacher, Miss Lachenal, on duty and stationed at the blackboard, cranked out the present indicative endings to French regular -er verbs: *-e, -es, -e, -ons, -ez, -ent.* Left of a tall curly left bracket containing the vertical stack of endings was the infinitive: *aimer*—to love, to like. Left of the verb and left of a tall curly right bracket were the nominative personal pronouns: *je, tu, il/elle/on, nous, vous, ils/elles.* I love is j'aime, we love is nous aimons, and so on. She spoke aloud as she wrote, careful to emphasize the z-like liaison between the final consonant of *nous* with the beginning vowels of the *aimons.* She didn't rush. I liked that. Each syllable, each sound got its proper share of space and time.

My French learning experience with Jean DeLambert, who though patient as a saint while cliffside, had been otherwise less-than-saintly. The uninterrupted rapidity with which he spoke French pureed the words into non-recognition.

I eased the door closed in dread of a creak that didn't materialize and checked things out. A pineapple farm of pimply-faced classmates faced me. And then there was the sun-like blinding presence of Miss Lachenal. The back of a black pencil skirt profiled two undulating bumps and the defile betwixt them. A starched, untucked shirttail stuck up like the skut of a white-tailed deer.

I'd seen deer at Devil's Lake. I plucked the word out of my puréed French—un cerf, from a memory embedded in a moment of motorized panic when DeLambert nearly slaughtered a family of deer socializing in the middle of the road.

I had to find a seat, right away.

I looked at my sneakers. Her spiked heels snapped at the floor and the chalk scraped the blackboard. A violent gust of wind precipitated a pressure drop. A branch whipped the windowpane and shed yellowed elm leaves. The pineapple heads twisted in unison toward the window. Miss Lachenal's gaze locked on me. She continued lecturing without pause and nodded at me to take a seat. No condemnation, no arrogance, none of that uppity shit you see when you're late for a class. I'd expected that sort of treatment because I was habitually late and never for any good reason. She'd learn.

I walked to the back of the room. There were maybe twenty-five kids in class. They were crammed in desks sized for students two grades younger. I selected a desk in the back row. There was one free seat abutting Miss Lachenal's desk, but I didn't want to be front-and-center. I knew I'd be late again and it was better to plan for it now. Next to me in the back and in the same row sat Mr. E. I had no idea what the hell he was doing here. He'd been my teacher for honors English last year. "Shit," I said. Heads turned. Not his.

My very first day of English class with Mr. E., in front of everybody, he announced that I was going to get a B, not an A. I gave him that classic teen look of incredulity and innocence and opened my arms, palms up. I'd been pronounced guilty without a trial. Or even a crime! *Unfair!*, my expression screamed. "Whaaat?" I said aloud.

One day I gave him some lip. It was an argument about platypuses only being in Australia. I told him they were in Tasmania, too, and that he didn't know what the hell he was talking about. He didn't respond, verbally, that is. He just walked over and clocked me on the head. I scanned the room for witnesses. Mr. E. Had not used his flesh and blood hand. He used the other one, the one where the forearm and hand was this Captain Hook affair, a wooden stump attached at the elbow and a sickle-shaped steel pincer for a hand. I never saw how it stuck on because he wore long-sleeve shirts, navy blue or white. The blow was no love tap. I watched my classmates eyes grow big and mouths drop. Not a word, no one dared. Me neither.

We became friends—even though later that first day he publicly announced that I was a "goddamned brown-nose" and that it'll be good for me to know what it's like to get a B. He wasn't bullshitting. He did give me a B even though I got an A on every damned assignment. He pissed me off, but I shut up and took it. I never complained—that, he respected.

Mr. E. swore a lot in class. He distributed humiliation freely and was fond of sending girls home if they dressed like "jailbait." I thought that was harsh as hell, but he stood up for the girls, too. There was always a feeling that Mr. E had your back. You felt it the second you walked through the door. The kids respected him and nobody, including the principal, messed with him. He and Miss Lachenal were friends.

He was in Lachenal's class that day because of some service requirement, one of those drills where teachers evaluate their colleagues. As I dropped my pack under my desk Mr. E. rose from his. The small desk lifted with him and then crashed back to the floor when he squeezed out of it. Lachenal stopped writing and looked our way. Mr. E.'s claw reached toward my head and pinched my ear. It hurt like the dickens. He didn't have much control over the pressure—it was all or nothing, a single setting to hold anything from an anvil to my ear lobe. Next, Mr. E. paraded me to the desk in the front row. I grabbed my pack and obediently followed. Miss Lachenal said nothing.

"You own this seat," he said. "You own it for the rest of the year."

Mr. E. unclamped my throbbing red ear. I felt the earlobe to see if it was bleeding. He turned to Miss Lachenal, "Well, back to work . . ." and headed out the door.

"Thanks, Mike," she answered. There was no discussion about my displacement, no sympathy either.

Miss Lachenal continued the lecture seated at her desk. I watched her, from up-close now. How could I ignore her? It was like we were having dinner together. I saw that her lipstick had run beyond the lips at one corner of her mouth. Not by much, maybe a sixteenth-of-an-inch. Her hair was straw-colored and cut short. It was thin, too, a lot thinner than the never-combed thicket on my head. I picked out an individual hair and traced it to the follicle in her scalp. It was darker at the root. That's how close I was to her.

Her crispy-white oxford was buttoned askew. She had missed a button at the waist. The flesh showed when she twisted to the right or reached with her right arm. Skin on her tummy was darker than the skin on her face or her hands. Maybe it appeared darker because of the contrast with the white cotton. Breasts, each a half-pear that would fit perfectly under my cupped hand, played hide and seek under white planes of fabric and a minimalist brassiere.

I'm more than okay with small breasts. Buddy Vlacek often opined about women's breasts, speaking with faux authority just like he did about his ram-rod pecker. He averred that bigger was better. Per Vlacek, I couldn't relate to what he was talking about since I was retarded about sex, retarded in several senses—less advanced in social and physical development and not so smart. He had a point: I'd never spent quality time with a girl's breasts, never. So far it had been a series of touch-and-goes. Set the wheels on the tarmac for second, then off you go. I was curious.

From the back of the classroom Miss Lachenal's eyes had been two-dimensional brownish disks. From here, a couple feet away, her eyes were vortices of green and gold and ringed with black coronas. The more I stared at her eyes, the more her body shrank into that Papa-Bear-sized desk and chair. She sat erect, posture perfect, her pointy sit-bones defibrillating the wooden plank under her butt. Did that farted-upon for generations and taken for granted chair seat know how lucky it was? And did Miss Lachenal have two little bruises on her bottom at day's end? These were the sort of profound questions that dogged my adolescent brain.

My skinny ass sure got sore sitting at a desk and she was as skinny as me. And not much older either. There were senior girls that definitely looked older than Miss Lachenal. I had so many questions. Why had Mr. E. dragged me up here?

"Bonjour." She popped to life-size and spoke to me.

"Hi," I said.

She scrutinized the class list, then me. I reddened.

"Bonjour, vous êtes Otto?"

I nodded.

"Bienvenue! This is your first French class, oui?"

"Yeah."

"Bon. I am Miss Lachenal. You may call me Mademoiselle Lachenal."

These days the French use Madame and never say "Mademoiselle." Old fogies and pervs get away with Mademoiselle but that's about it. In 2012 the French even banished Mademoiselle from official forms and registries. I heard an exception was made for some stockpiled forms that were too expensive to reprint. Quelle surprise! French shopkeeper mentalité trumps political correctness! I'm not anti-feminist, but this Mademoiselle thing was an overreaction. Especially for a nation that takes such pride in its linguistic heritage.

She rose. The chair sighed as she reached across the desk and shook my hand. I appreciated the adult acknowledgment and firm handshake. Mlle Lachenal was petite, but wiry strong like me.

"Mr. E. likes you," she said.

Seemed like everybody called him Mr. E., though I had noted the familiar "Mike" when he had left the room. I had been told but had forgotten his actual name. It was something like Scorpion, which made no sense at all.

"He's got a funny way of showing it." I rubbed my sore and hot red ear.

"Where did you take French 1?"

"I didn't. That is, I didn't take a class. But I learned from someone."

"Not here?"

"No."

"Can you come to my office after class? Let's make sure this is the right class for you. I don't want you to have to repeat material you already know, or be in over your head. Does that work?"

". . . ça marche bien, merci." That works, I said, showing off a little.

She smiled and returned to the lesson and the blackboard.

The desk in her office was faded blond and the same vintage as the one in the classroom. She sat on the corner of the desk as I lowered into the chair facing her. If anything, we were physically closer than in the classroom. I smelled her perfume, or maybe the cut roses in the vase. Whatever the aroma, it gave me this heady feeling.

I looked at the roses. "From Mr. E.?"

"Mais, oui!" she said. "How did you know they were from him?"

"He's talked about rose bushes in his backyard. He's got, like, a greenhouse. That's his hobby: growing rose trees or bushes, whatever they are. That's how he hurt his arm, doing something in the garden."

She leaned back and made a sort of half-snort, half-laugh. I watched her skirt crawl up over her knees as her legs swung back and forth like a little kid's, moving without cadence.

"He told you that?!"

"Yeah?" I wondered why the doubt.

"Oh, I shouldn't say—but I will."

She paused and then leaned forward, arms spread out to either side and hands gripping the edge of the desk like she was about to launch off of it to attack me. Her shirt wasn't tucked in anymore. I could see out the gap I had peeked into before.

"He lost his forearm on the Omaha Beachhead. He was in the U.S. 1st Infantry Division. Do you know about Omaha Beachhead?"

I didn't, so Mlle Lachenal explained in some detail the landing on that eight-kilometer strip of beach in Normandy on D-Day, June 6, 1944. That landing was part of the largest seaborne invasion in history. Of course I knew about the war, but the conversation with Mlle Lachenal hit me in the gut; what a complete shit-show war was and what an immeasurable waste of life it entailed. That brief conversation with her has never left me. At times, it sustained me. As did the memory of Mr. E.'s courage.

Her eyes got watery and her nose ran. Instead of a handkerchief, she rubbed her shirtsleeve under her nose. A damp splotch marked the cuff.

"I was ten when my father disappeared from my life. He was from Normandy. Spoke French, English, and German. He had been part of Operation Jedburgh. In the middle of the night he was dropped by parachute into occupied France . . . and vanished. They never found him. Never found his body. Nothing."

The smile wilted. She was trying to keep the corners of her mouth from tipping downward. The effort made her jaw quiver like a winter leaf on a naked branch, a leaf spared detachment but drained of life.

I forgot about looking down her blouse and stepped toward her, moving to comfort on instinct. She hopped off the desk and embraced me. I was taller and she nestled under my left arm and squeezed hard. I was too surprised to hug back. She heaved a couple of times and little shudders moved through her body and into mine. Her breathing evened out. I closed my eyes, rested my cheek against the top of her head. Her chest widened and contracted. Breasts and stomach relaxed against my hip and leg.

She eased away from me, her hands still on my shoulders. "Je suis désolé, sorry. That wasn't appropriate."

"Tant pis," I said.

The look on Mlle Lachenal's face flashed hurt and anger. She moved closer—like eye-to-eye. Tension came and went.

"What do you *think* you said?" she asked in full teacher mode.

"Tant pis," I repeated.

"In English, Otto. What do you think you said in English?"

"I don't know. 'It'll be okay.' I mean I don't think and translate. I just say stuff that feels right, like what should come next."

"Well, that's good. That's very good, in fact. But this time your gut lead you astray. Tant pis means 'too bad' or 'whatever.' It decidedly does not mean 'it'll be okay.' In fact, it's rude. One could say 'ça ira.' "

"Shit. I'm sorry. I didn't—" I really did feel sorry, and stupid, and embarrassed. I was full-on red in the face.

"Ça ira!" she said. She gave me a chaste little hug and a smile. "That expression dates back to a song from the French Revolution, a song written in 1792." I think she said that to distract me from my embarrassment.

She paused and peered up at me, like she was sizing me up. "Otto." I smelled her breath. It was adult breath, end of the work-day breath. With an adult body odor to go with it. "You'll be fine in my class."

We looked at each other. I said, "Thank you." I said "Thank you" several times, in fact. I didn't know why. But I knew I wasn't only thanking her for meeting with me about class.

Nager: / na.ʒe / verb / to swim

Zoom 5

"Mom said school was hard, not easy for you? Like you didn't finish high school."

"Zadie, dear, don't be a pest. Maybe the rest of the family isn't as curious as you are. Papa Otto has been polite, but I don't think he really wants to talk about high school. If he even remembers!"

Was Kali was giving me an out? A way to avoid saying something I'd regret or something hurtful.

I had no intention of breaking the rules. A deal's a deal. I stay out of my family's hair. They're happy and I'm happy. Or not. What did Graham Greene write? "In human relationships, kindness and lies are worth a thousand truths."

Ah, fuck it. "Your mom is the one who doesn't remember. I left at the end of my junior year. I didn't fill out the paperwork for graduation, but I had enough credits. A year or so later, the school classified me as having graduated early. My old French teacher made it happen."

"You had a crush on her, didn't you! Did you stay in touch with her after your third year?"

"Sort of," I waffled.

"Sort of hmmmm . . ." Zadie was turning on the charm. "Sort of what?"

"Sort of taught her to swim."

Zadie grunted an "Uh huh," as if this was exactly the response she had expected.

Silence ruled until Kali salvoed: "Otto. Please don't make up stuff." Then to Zadie, "Don't listen to him, honey. I never heard a word about this until now and I should know."

"I never mentioned it until now!" I was offended and let it be known.

"Tell me, Papa Otto!" Is discord unhealthy for teens? Zadie thrived on it. "Did you or didn't you?"

Kali backpeddled, seeing the possibility that there might be some truth in what I had said. I was relieved Zadie hadn't pursued the 'crush' question. "Papa Otto was a lifeguard at the 16th Street public pool. Was your teacher in a swim class?"

"Well done, Kali! Great guess."

The Kiss

And dead wrong.

The last day of my junior year was the class picnic. It wasn't a school-wide event. The logistics would have been impossible given the size of the student body. The picnickers comprised students from select language classes and a handful of teachers. All of the students were seniors except me. The location was somewhere among the Chain O'Lakes, a dozen or so small lakes connected by the Fox River and less than an hour's drive from Cicero.

The place was nowhere near as cool as Devil's Lake. Instead of pink bluffs, shaded woods, log cabins, a dance hall and a spring-fed lake you could drink out of, Chain O'Lakes was dead flat and surrounded by cow-pied fields. Drink that water and you'd shit like a cow. There was a tacky plastic waterpark and a couple of neoned burger joints. A lakeside shop sold worms for spinner-types (forget fly-fishing!) and rented paddle boats and canoes without any of that waiver nonsense.

I spent most of the time shuffling around and not-talking to the other kids. I didn't socialize well; still don't. At the end of the day, around three, an hour before we had to return to the school buses, Mlle Lachenal took my arm and guided me toward the lake. We chatted, a little in French, more in English. I told her I was sad to be finished with her class and that I had no idea what I was going to do over the summer or next year or the rest of my life.

We passed a boathouse and dock with canoes one could take out on the lake. The wall behind the caretaker was covered with photos of speedboats, but I hadn't seen a single one on the lake. This wasn't much of a lake, and I couldn't imagine a speedboat having enough room to, well, speed.

The thought of everyone overhearing the what-does-the-future-hold-for-me talk with Mlle Lachenal did not appeal to me, so I asked her if she'd like to go for a paddle. She declined at first. I said nothing and then for whatever reason she changed her mind. Maybe she saw how small the lake was, how small I was, and the grand, looming uncertainty of the future I faced.

"Pourquoi pas! Why not. I've never been in a canoe. Have you?"

"Lots," I lied. I had seen canoes at Devil's Lake and figured that if one of those hoods-in-the-woods idiots could manage a canoe, so could I.

I'd watched Do-gooder Counselor climb into a canoe. I did what he had done. I eased my weight onto one foot on the centerboard, brought my other foot onboard without shifting around, and slowly lowered into the seat near the stern of the canoe. The canoe tipped slightly as I sat because the center of gravity of my ass wasn't exactly the same as my feet. I made a quick correction, looked up, and was relieved that Mlle Lachenal had turned away momentarily and missed the miscue. She stepped closer and squatted like catcher waiting for a fastball. The floating dock wobbled.

Mlle Lachenal was wearing a teacher-appropriate sleeveless white tee and a pair of khaki culottes. I always thought the word was "kulaks," for Russian peasants. Not so. Culottes, are any sort of pants, shorts, or panties or boxers. A "culot" is the lower half of anything. The 60s culottes Mlle Lachenal sported were baggy shorts with wide cuffs and oversized pockets. In the 60s, women's pants had real pockets.

She handed the paddle to me. Still in a squat—I don't how she managed this—she slipped a foot out of one sneaker, then out of the other, and gamely tossed the shoes into the belly of the boat.

She looked fit, like she could hold a Malasana pose for an hour or do five-hundred squats. Her crotch was eye-level. I'd been there before. I once dropped my pencil to the floor so I could lean over and peek up her skirt. That might sound perverted. I guess it was. I think I was curious more than anything else. I fantasized that Mlle Lachenal knew what I was doing and spread her legs so I could get a better look, like Eve handing the apple to Adam. When I surfaced, I realized that I'd been holding my breath.

The canoe shifted under us. Her fingers choked the gunwale. The gunwale's that strip of wood that runs around the boat and along the top edge of the hull. It seemed odd, Mlle Lachenal being nervous. A crescent of sweat, like an earring, hung under each armhole of her sleeveless tee. Maybe she was hot. My ego argued that she was excited about being with me. My intelligence said dream on, dude. Was she breaking a school regulation? Would she get in trouble? Am I going to get her in trouble?

"You sure this is okay?" I asked. "You know, you and me? *Ensemble.*"

"Oui, oui. Pas de problème." She coughed out a nervous laugh and put on a pair of Holly Golightly sunglasses she had had in her pocket.

Okay, I thought. No problem. Of course not. She wasn't the squeamish type. One day she'd brought a real calf brain to class so we could talk about it in French. Ask yourself, how many French teachers do *that*!

I kept one hand on the dock and steadied the boat with the other as she got in. Mlle Lachenal crawled monkey-like to the faux-caned seat at the bow. She was lighter than me, so even though I wasn't at the very stern of the canoe, the craft sat level in the water. A gentle push off the dock and voilà, we drifted into open water. The air was calm, the water calmer. The sounds of workers and of families playing and yelling diminished as we distanced ourselves from the landing. The canoe rippled the surface of the water. The alternating dribble and silence of the paddling marked our progress. So did Mlle Lachenal's breathing. Short breaths in, longer controlled breaths out. I felt her gaze grazing my shoulder and fixed upon the shore. Every so often she would inspect the bottom of the canoe. She hardly moved, her hands glued to the gunwale on either side of the seat, her back erect.

"Look, a fish!" I pointed to a bass just under the surface.

Mlle Lachenal didn't stir.

We'd gone perhaps a hundred-fifty yards offshore and still not a word. Felt romantic, sharing the silence like that. And weird too, because she was so stiff.

Finally, she spoke: "Otto. I want to go back."

I paddled one stroke more toward the open water.

"Now," she said. "I want to go back now."

I nodded and switched to paddling on only one side so we would do a half-circle. I even managed that tricky thing of leaving the paddle in the water at the end of the stroke to act as a rudder. Her head didn't rotate. She stared straight at me. I figured this was my cue, the moment I had hoped for since the hug in her office on day one of class.

I carefully placed the paddle alongside my feet and rose from my seat. The canoe felt stable enough for me to work my way forward. Mlle Lachenal saw what was going to happen before I did. I saw the reflection in the oversized lenses of her sunglasses—the stern of the canoe rose out of the water behind me like the head and neck of the Loch Ness monster. Mlle Lachenal lunged toward me in an attempt to rebalance the boat. She wasn't thinking the same thing I had been thinking.

The boat tilted and skewed to one side. I lost my balance. Mlle Lachenal lurched forward and I fell into her. The stern made a sucking sound as it peeled off of the water and rose skyward.

"Otto!" Mlle Lachenal screamed as we tumbled into the warm lake water.

She wrapped her arms around my shoulders, then around my head, like she wanted to pushed me under and drown me. I didn't get it. I dove and opened my eyes. Her legs and feet were flailing. She kicked me in the face. It wasn't intentional and I don't think she even knew what she'd done.

I'm half fish and really at home in the water. I swam under and resurfaced behind her and then wrapped an arm around her chest. Her head fell back against my shoulder.

"—du calme." I repeated the phrase several times. To further reassure her that she was not in danger, I pressed my head against hers. Her hair was in my mouth. Water was in my mouth.

"—sais pas nager!"

"Pas nager" means "not swim." She didn't know how to swim!

The boat had filled with water. Idiot that I was, I didn't know that most canoes float and even full of water you could paddle a canoe to China. I assumed we'd have to swim to shore. I slipped a finger into the back of each of my shoes and let them sink to the bottom. With one arm snugged up under her breasts, I side-stroked toward shore. She coughed and spit up water off and on, but eventually her body relaxed and floated along. The water was warm, our bodies were warm, and we had adjusted to the rhythmic mingling of thighs and feet and torsos. Stroke-by-stroke the gap between us and land lessened. The panic subsided and she started breathing with me.

Even after our feet touched the muddy bottom she clung to my side, under my arm like that first hug, and let me help her ashore. We sloshed out of the water, leaning into each other until we reached the grassy high ground. Mlle Lachenal's eyes were popping with life. The sunglasses had been lost. A half-laugh became a gag. She leaned forward and spat.

Still hanging off my arm, she raised a hand to her face and cleared her nose. I don't know why but the act gave us the giggles. A gang of kids gathered around to see what was so funny. Our clothes sucked flat to our skin. When we tried to peel the soggy fabric off our stomachs it flopped back with a splat. My gut hurt from laughing. When Mlle Lachenal got hold of herself, she took my face in both hands and kissed me, giving me a sloppy, slobbering smacker right on the lips. The crowd cheered. I raised two fists to the sky and grinned 'til it hurt.

Enceinte: / ã. sɛ̃t / adjective / pregnant

Zoom 6

"A crush! That's so sweet. You were—."

"No big lesson, Zades." I thought it best to shut down the inquiry. I do respect Zadie's curiosity. But her coming-of-age story was a lot more complicated than mine. If she was looking for perspective, my experience, being so predictably straight, might send the wrong message. I couldn't imagine the courage it would take to question one's sexual identity—at her age or any age.

"Last I ever saw of her," I lied. "End of crush, end of story. Sorry." It sounded sad and it was sad. It wasn't just a crush. Not then, not after a year, not after twenty years, not now. Do we ever not love someone once loved, after their memory has made a homestead in the heart?

Kali donned the emcee hat. A few of the aunts and uncles, cousins and the like were keen to return to their respective Thanksgiving events and weary of the Zadie-Otto exchange. As a rule, the family members were a selfish lot. Or maybe selfish was the wrong word. They simply weren't interested in anything beyond their own noses and what Fox News told them.

Kali organized the diaspora and, one-by-one, half of the tiles on the screen went dark. She handheld the tech-illiterate through the process. None of the departed said goodbye to me. That's how invisible we were to each other.

The dematerialization of the aged: we are seen only by the very young, the very old, loved ones, and scanners at the airport, and scammers who want our money. I'm not going to journal our descent into translucence and inevitable nothingness. Wallace Stegner's been there, done that in Spectator Bird *and* Angle of Repose. *I hope he didn't really feel that shitty about aging. Truth is, I don't think about age much. I like my social security check and VA benefits. And I love my Eagle Pass for the National Parks, the best deal ever. When I purchased mine, it was only ten bucks.*

"In college," Zadie pressed on, "did you study French in college?"

"Sort of," I said.

"What's that mean? Your giving me the 'sort of' treatment again!"

"How about—yes."

"Did you take books home?"

"I did, I did." I said that twice to convey the burden the experience had entailed. "I studied French the following year at Cornell."

"In New York?"

"No, I wish. Or maybe I don't. This was the CORNell—Mt. Vernon, Iowa. With a capital C. O. R. N."

"I thought you were in Colorado?"

"Cornell was before Colorado. Our next-door neighbor's kid went to school in Iowa, so when I told my folks I'd had it with high school, they said I could go to work or go to Cornell. Work is, well, work. So, I applied to Cornell, was accepted, and moved to Iowa. I *didn't know what I wanted but I knew what I didn't want—which was more high school or another minute in Cicero."*

"And you flunked out . . ." Kali knew this bits and pieces of the Cornell saga.

"And I flunked out . . ." I echoed. "But I learned a fuck-load of French."

"Otto!" Kali scolded.

"I know, I know."

Zadie's curiosity picked up. We even rekindled the interest of a few remaining family members who, like me, could relate to dropping out of college or had picked up the vulgarity. I could see their interest from their body language, even on Zoom. The **deplorables** *on my screen had had their share of failures and relished the failures of others.*

This time I preempted Zadie's question. "I went to classes. But there were . . . distractions."

"Boy or girl distractions?" Zadie jumped in.

She's fishing for direction on this sex thing, I thought. Maybe my ex talked about me being gay or on the fence. Certainly be one way to rationalize the divorce.

"Guilty as charged," I said. "It was a girl—or maybe both." The both part is complicated.

"More! Tell me more!"

I was on my third vodka on the rocks, splash of lime, thank you. Alcohol obviates unpleasant memories of tasteless wedding toasts, late night emails, and times we missed saying that one word that would have made a difference. The drinking helps little for major fuck-ups like the guilt and the recurring and unwelcome desire to set the record straight. It's a rare day goes by when some nasty memory doesn't raise a hind leg and piss on me.

But this chronicle is about how I learned French; it is not a confessional. And neither you, my reader, nor you, Zadie, are my father confessor or my bartender.

There was a bit of settling in, scene setting, before tackling the Cornell experience. Not that I would ever fully reveal what had transpired.

"Cornell was—probably still is—a small school," I said. "The student body was a fifth the size of my high school's. The entire population of Mt. Vernon was under five thousand, probably still is today. It was the paradigm small college town. The average age was in the low twenties, probably a third of the residents were affiliated with the college. The town had six resident cops and four resident sex offenders. Was that a tipping point?"

"Otto—" Kali interrupted, but I pressed on with the setting, still uncertain about what I was and wasn't going to report. What was that word for parents like my daughter Kali—hoverers, helicopters? How could a laissez-fair father like me have created a heli-parent?

"Mt. Vernon had double the number of fatal road traffic accidents as the rest of Iowa. Don't know, but I expect the town had twice as much sex as the rest of Iowa—farm critters excepted."

Kali groaned, "Jesus, Otto!"

"So?" Zadie said, ignoring or inured to the reference to bestiality. I bet there's a YouTube site devoted to sex with animals. Kids probably look at it for a minute, are bored, and move on with life.

"Yes, she was a friend, a friend I cherished and protected."

Zadie placed hands to bosom, and wanting to or not, exhibited a surprising and public presentation of her feminine side.

"Guilty as charged." I said the words without thinking.

Zadie hit me point-blank: "Were you lovers?"

"Zades," I said, stalling for what to say, "she was pregnant. The child was NOT mine."

"Boy or girl?"

"Boy."

The diaspora had ended, the hangers-on were going to tough it out. Zadie was thinking. The new data was sinking in and I believe something in her knew better than to take her Papa Otto too far on this one. We have this intuitive respect for one another.

"I get it," she said, not knowing what "it" was. And then asked, "What's pregnant in French?"

"Enceinte. Comes from the Latin, to ungirt."

"Like in une ceinture—a belt? I read Sept d'un Coup, about the tailor who killed seven flies with one blow and embroidered the words on his belt."

I thought about the Grimm's fairy tale and the illusions we strew around us like seeds and how those seeds sprout roots and stalks and look for light . . .

Iowa

Cyrus cranked the wheel hard right and we careened onto State Highway 1. The tires chirped when the auto jerked from dirt to asphalt. I lost my footing on the rear bumper. One leg flailed in the air, the other stayed put on the chrome bumper. My left hand had a death grip on the trunk's mesh-like luggage rack. My right arm flailed in the air like a rodeo cowboy. This cowboy's hand, however, clutched an unlabeled bottle of Cyrus' homemade wine.

Where and how he made wine was a mystery. I'd asked, but he had this peculiar faculty for deflecting personal inquiries. I wondered how he would manage at his oral defense. Cyrus was soon to complete his doctorate in philosophy at the University of Iowa in Iowa City, another college burg about twenty miles south of Mt. Vernon and near to our current destination. Cyrus and I shared an unusual responsibility. But more about that later.

"Don't drop the damned wine!" The words bellowed out of cheeks distended by the wind. Our eyes tagged each other in a rearview mirror small enough to fit in a cosmetics bag.

The Austin-Healey, a mid-fifties vintage, ran topless. I never understood how Cyrus afforded the car since he lived on student loans. "Sir Healey" was gorgeous. He—the car was male —was a long-snouted two-seater with spoked wheels with spin-off hubs. The shape of the hood vent and oval grill gave the low-slung vehicle a permanent snarl. With a decent paint job, the car would have been handsome. Unfortunately for Sir Healey, instead of British racing green, the car wore a coat of rust-splotched aqua. A lone driving light mounted on the front bumper driver's side stared at the ground and longed for a mate.

In the rubbed raw and tattered bucket seat beside Cyrus sat Carol Conner-Baker. Her blonde ringlets uncoiled and recoiled as Cyrus pushed Sir Healey—seventy, eighty, then ninety miles per hour. Cyrus was lanky as a cornstalk and had silky tufts of hair above the ears. His prematurely bald pate was speckled and sunburnt. He drove with the nonchalant insouciance of a wannabe James Dean, elbow on the doorsill and the tips of two bony fingers guiding the wheel. The other arm alternated between resting on the back of the passenger seat and stabbing the shift knob for gear changes. Occassionally, a crosswind snagged his wire-rimmed glasses and he'd let go the wheel to reposition them.

Carol grabbed my wrist and I scrunched into turtle-pose. She took the jug and put it between her feet, avoiding the cardboard covered hole in the sheet metal floorboard. The wind made it impossible to speak. Our mouths formed ghoulish grins.

Cyrus cranked the wheel right and Sir Healey drifted sideways. Gravel sprayed the air when the rear tires touched the pebbled surface. Our driver corrected the slide as we sidled up to a drainage ditch parallel to the road. We pretended that this had not been a dangerous maneuver. No one was wearing seatbelts.

"There's where we're headed!" He pointed to a tree off in the distance. We slowed. The wind racket abated.

Two minutes later, at the identified tree, I peeled stiff fingers from the luggage rack. The skin on my face and arms tingled from windburn. I felt dust and a taunt dryness on the surface of my eyes and in my throat.

Cyrus stood on the seat and hopped over the driver's door. "Pop the boot," he ordered.

I unwound the baling wire securing the lid of the trunk, reached in and retrieved a Julie Andrews worthy picnic basket: baloney sandwiches, Velveeta cheese, extra mayo, and a pink Tupperware container labeled "petits fours" but filled with Oreos. There were two one-liter bottles of Perrier and paper cups. A bag of chips lay next to the basket. Paper cups were strewn across the floor of the trunk.

"So, Chanel—" That was Curtis's pet name for Carol. It is a girl's name and means "canal" in English—hence, insulting à la Shakespeare. "A little vino, folks?"

"Pour moi, non!" she said.

"Wine?" he asked me.

"Sure," I said

Cyrus turned to Carol. "To Bobo!"

That pet name was the one he used for the little human residing in Carol's uterus. Cyrus had pet names for everything. Bobo was French for boo-boo. I learned later that it also meant "bourgeois bohème." We never settled on the pronunciation. Sometimes it was with "oo" and sometimes with a long "o." Cyrus was *not* the father. I'd seen the real father only once. Carol had pointed him out one night. He'd been stalking her. We ducked into the school library to hide.

The guy scared the shit out of me. He was way bigger than me, maybe six-three or four to my five-ten. Mister Stalker was solid muscle and had a male model five o'clock shadow. You knew that, even after shaving, a swarthy yin-yang imprint would remain on his face. Carole said Jock was a French-Canadian lumberjack. You'd think he would go by Jacques . . . but no, it was plain old Jock. I'd read bits and pieces of Diderot's *Jacques le fataliste et son maître*. Jock was not a *Philosophe*.

The dude was incredibly handsome. Probably that's why she'd fucked him. Carol said she'd been drunk, and it had been a one-night stand. But after I saw the guy, how handsome he was, I think Carol made up the being drunk part and lost count after that. The affair must have gone on for several months. Carol and I were in French conversation group and over a period of a couple of months I'd noticed the bruises come and go on her face and arms. Once her lip was split and so swollen that she couldn't speak. Right after that session, I stopped going to my regular classes. Carol had grabbed me by the arm and walked us down a hall, staying about twenty feet behind our French professor. We loitered outside his office door until the hallway had emptied.

"Did anyone see you?" the professor asked Carol. Then he looked at me. "Who's he?"

"Silly ass, he's in your class."

That was not exactly the way I talked to my professors. Must be okay if you're a senior and an honor student.

"Mon Dieu! I'm so upset about all this. Please, forgive me." The guy was apologizing to me. That was a first. College was different than high school.

I gave him time to search for my name, then spoke. "Hey, it's okay. I don't remember your name either."

I didn't—truly—so I said mine: "Otto."

"Doctor Clarence DeBrique." He half-rose but stopped short of a handshake.

"I need another bodyguard," Carol said, "if we're serious about someone being with me twenty-four seven. That was the deal. Full-time coverage or officer Iona's going to make me leave campus. I will NOT let that happen. I'm graduating, I'm going to grad school next year, and I'm having this damned baby."

That was a shocker, the baby. She was a little fat. Food here wasn't bad and I'd put on a few pounds.

The professor puffed out his chest. A little tuft of fluff stuck out from his pudgy goat face. I had not even started shaving yet. I was super slow at developing, like the bottom of the bottom ten percent. My mom had been so worried she spoke with our family doc. He came for dinner and told me to eat more. In those days, we had a real family doctor who made house calls.

"I'll cancel morning classes. This is my responsibility." He flattened double-jointed fingers over the top of the desk and ignoring me, continued. "As my mistress, Carol, your well-being is my responsibility!"

Carol walked around the desk and bumped him to the side with her hip. She flopped down in the leather chair that retained an imprint of his buttocks. "You are a dear, Clarence, but I am not *your* mistress or anybody else's!"

"I won't—"

"Come *on*, Clarence. It's not the 1800s; we're not in France, though your French is lovely. Anyway, chase your little boys—"

A furtive glace followed to see if I'd heard. Of course, I had. Did I care if he was a perv—it struck me as kinda sick if it was true. Anyway, I wasn't about to announce it over the PA system. I pretended to be interested just to spook him. The guy had victim written across his face. He wouldn't last a minute on the West Side.

"Unfair, Carol. Please, don't even suggest that." He turned and looked at me, all earnest: "Of course, that was in jest."

"My well-intentioned and less than pragmatic guardian," Carol went on like she was auditioning for *Taming of the Shrew*, "you have a jealous wife, two children, and a real job. You do not have time for me and I do need another bodyguard —man or woman. And, yes, a sweet, young boy like Otto will do."

The professor regarded me with a sort of haughty distrust. "He is really in college? He looks like a first-year high schooler!"

I was worried that he was sizing me up for you know what.

"He's tougher than he looks, trust me."

I agreed with Carol on that point. I'd had this guy for a couple months of classes and only met him in person today, but, like I'd said, he was a chicken-shit. I'm not. Chicago teaches you real fast about who's got balls and who doesn't. Jock, on the other hand, radiated serial killer.

Clarence pleaded with Carol. "Mon petit chou, I adore, you!"

"Shoe?" That did sound like something a perv would say.

"Cabbage," Carol translated.

Even grosser, I thought.

Carol's voice got all flirty, quoting from *Madame Bovary*: "... le charme de la nouveauté, peu à peu tombant comme un vêtement, laissait voir à nu l'éternelle monotonie de la passion."

"Am I to understand that I bore you?"

"Clarence," she touched his forearm, "I still need your help, and I sincerely appreciate your letting me use your office. But no sex, c'est fini." The *fini* she spoke with her head down, as if she were talking to the desk. After she looked up, so they were face to face again, she continued. "So's your wife. Tired of it— the 'it' being you and me and the fucking and all behind her back."

"She doesn't know."

"Dear, I can smell her pussy on that noisome little beard of yours. And she can smell mine."

He froze, now glued to the conversation. Wow, Carol could sure make a point.

"She knows. Accept and be grateful. She's nice, and we feel guilty as shit. Get her a new Kitchen-Aid mixer, read the underwear catalog in the bathroom when you have to, and be the good hubby. No, that's condescending—the bit about the mixer, not you on the can. Be a real man and apologize to her."

I'd heard enough to get that I shouldn't be a part of this conversation. "I think I'll go—"

They both reached out for me and I jumped back. I was quick and they missed.

"No!" Carol ordered.

"Attends!" from the professor. That utterance, of course, stopped me dead in my tracks.

I planted my feet, one hand on the door, and waited for an explanation. It came forthwith.

"Otto," Carol addressed me like this was a marriage proposal, "Will you be my bodyguard?"

"Bodyguard?"

"Yes. Remember that man I pointed out to you—"

"Jock, yeah," I answered.

"He's crazy. He's the father of the child I'm carrying."

She let her tummy protrude and caressed it with her hands, telegraphing something I'd already figured out.

"Even though he's the father, he wants to hurt me. Possibly kill me."

That, I hadn't figured out. "Seriously?"

"Quite seriously. Because I won't marry him and God told him that that was a grievous sin. A worse sin than killing me."

"That's pretty fucked-up logic." I wanted clarification.

"For me to have his child without marrying him. I deserve to die. For tricking him into getting me pregnant. I deserve to die. For having a child that is now Satan's fetus, not his. I deserve to die. The child as well."

"Yeah, well that's totally crazy and scary as shit," I said.

"I've been able to stay with either Clarence or Cyrus. Cyrus helps. But, I don't have a car, so it's hard for Cyrus. He has to go back and forth from Iowa city so I can be here for my classes. And Clarence's wife, she's been away but she's back tomorrow."

"I live in a dorm," I explained.

"I know," she said. "I know your RA. He won't care."

"The school will find out."

"They'll ignore it. Officer Iona, the sheriff, will ignore it too. He's the one who suggested I stay on campus. My apartment is on the edge of town. The creep knows where it is and I wouldn't be safe there. It's not like they've got cops to spare."

"The creep, Jock, looks mean."

"He's meaner than he looks."

"Can't officer Iona arrest him?"

"Not really. He's hit me. But it's a 'he says she says case.' And Jock never misses church and never says the crazy shit he says to me to anyone else. Besides, I don't want everybody to know I'm pregnant."

One of her eyes twitched. Little beads of sweat gathered around her hairline. She was stressed. Afraid.

I thought about Mr. E. at Omaha beachhead and when our class performed Julius Caesar. I was Brutus. *There is a tide in the affairs of men / Which, taken at the flood, leads on to fortune.* I figured this was my moment to step up, so I did.

"Okay. I'll be your bodyguard. I can do it."

"You sure?" Carol asked again even though I had just told her I would.

Her pause gave me pause. Instead of Mr. E., I thought about *Jacques le fataliste* and Jacques' conviction that life was pre-determined. And I thought about the nature of a commitment like this. What the hell do I know about being a bodyguard? My thoughts were jumping on top of each other.

I made an attempt to convince myself. "Yup. Absolutely."

"I love you love you love you!" She shot a flurry of air-kisses my way and hopped up and down with her hands holding her tummy. "You'll have to put up with me. Not when I'm at classes; but a lot. And I can study at Clarence's office or the library. Nights and weekdays, you're stuck with me. Cyrus picks me up most weekends. It's really okay?"

"Yup." My mind was made up. "What about the guys in the dorm?"

She winked. "They'll get used to it."

And they did. My male dorm-mates took her presence in stride. She never explained why she moved into my room, but it was clear I was watching over her and the rest of dorm rolled with it. Even Jock would have had his hands full if he busted into the place. Several students were Iowa farm boys who'd been baling hay since they were twelve. And Carol made it easy for them. She used the guys' bathroom and swore, farted, and dumped with the best of them. When she showered, they mostly gave her privacy. I was blown away. I'd always assumed that my dormies were a bunch of dorks, but they were okay.

A side effect to the new regimen was that I flunked out. There was no way to both make up my lost classes and guard Carol between hers. I hung out or read next to the door like a dog waiting for its master. When the weather improved, I'd wait outside the building. Some classes, like Professor DeBricke's Advanced French Lit, I joined her even though I only half-understood what was taught and discussed. He knew my name now and made me feel like I was part of the class.

Weekends I hung with her and Cyrus, which is how I ended up at the picnic, lying under the tree.

A voice whispered: "Big question, Otto."

I was on my back with my head on Carol's lap. She was scratching my scalp with her nails. The back and forth of her fingers in my hair made me sleepy. It wasn't sexual. We'd never talked about sex. At least I hadn't. I'm a freshman and look like I'm sixteen and she was six or seven months along. After living together for three months, we'd fallen into an easy routine.

She leaned over my head. "Otto?"

We were eye to sideways eye. I missed what she had said.

"Yeah?"

"I want to go to the graduation dance."

"Cool," I said and turned to Cyrus. "You dance, right."

"Nary a step," he said.

"Cyrus dear will be away. In San Francisco with his folks."

"Too bad," I said. Still not getting her drift. I can be slow.

"You'll be my date, won't you?"

I was in this half-dream already, "Why not."

"Do *you* dance?" she asked.

This sounded more like a high-school prom than a college affair, but remember, Cornell is a very small college and in a very small town.

"Sure," I replied. I was an okay dancer. After the car theft fiasco part of my rehab/punishment had been some hours of public service. Dance classes were an alternative, a better one than alternative public service gigs. I was pretty good at swing and enjoyed being good at something.

"You need a car," she said.

"I don't have a car."

"Can you borrow one?"

I looked at Cyrus.

"I'm driving to San Francisco."

"Maybe my dad's," I said. "I'd have to go home and see if I can use it for the weekend."

"I can pay for your bus back to Chicago."

"Why do I need a car?"

"The dance is three miles from the school, at The Barn. I don't want to ride the shuttle or go with anyone else. It's too—" She looked at her tummy—"too uncomfortable."

Carol was showing more. The bigger she got, the more the resentment there was about her pregnancy. After all, Cornell was a fucking Christian college. A gaggle of uncharitable believers resented the special treatment she'd received from the school administration, implying that her living in the guy's dorm would result in alums having second thoughts come check-writing time. The school president, who was going to retire at the end of the year, liked Carol and didn't give a shit about the Christian crusaders and buried their complaints.

Carol and I had had dinner with the president one night. He backed Carol's desire to finish her work. She's told me what her thesis topic was a half-dozen times. I always tuned it out. There's something so incredibly boring about someone talking about their big thesis, even Carol. Especially boring are the wannabes who never quite finished and now double-down about the increasingly fabricated circumstances that had prevented them from completing a doctorate.

I give Carol credit. The girl is no quitter; she gets shit done. I love that about her. Her undergrad thesis had been completed and submitted on time. She had been accepted by an Ivy League school and would jump straight into their doctoral program. The girl was a hell of a lot more sensible about her academic life than her personal one.

Fortunately, Cornell didn't post grades until after the end of the school year, so my parents had no idea about my dismal academic status. It took a while to sweet talk my folks out of the car. They gave in when I told them I would be coming home that weekend anyway so either they had to drive out to pick me up and load my junk in the car or they could let me take the car and I could manage the move on my own. I exaggerated how much personal crap I had and painted a picture of the three of us squeezed into the bench seat in front and massive sculpture from art class in the back seat and sticking out the window.

They resisted until I told them that the sculpture was a naked mermaid wearing a cowboy hat. Cyrus did have a life-sized, piñata-like mermaid that he'd bought at some second-hand store. She was frozen in a seated position. He'd strap her in the passenger seat of Sir Healey for long trips. Someone intelligent to talk to, he said.

My threat worked. Anyway, my mom was busy that weekend and Dad, who was half-blind, didn't relish the idea of driving anywhere unfamiliar.

The other consideration was my social life. Since I'd not said a word about Carol or Cyrus, or for that matter anybody else, it seemed like I had zero friends. Mom worried about my non-existent social life and was relieved when I told her I needed the car for a real date for the biggest event of the year, the school graduation dance. The car, I explained, was a prerequisite to getting the date. I went on about The Barn. Three miles grew to ten. Mom called the party the "prom." She did this, I think, to make up for the prom I had missed in high school. I liked giving her hope—it's what liars do, give people hope, especially people they love. With feigned reluctance, I described a freshman girl I'd had a crush on those first months at Cornell. Sharing the deeply-cultivated fantasy—I really had thought I was in love— made the lie that much more credible.

My once upon a time heartthrob's name was Dolly. She was short and compact, a pony-tailed and freckled frat-boy-chasing soon-to-be sorority girl. Two weeks into the school year she'd latched onto a tall, good-looking guy who could dance better than me. I was so jealous of the perfect couple. They were aloof, dismissive, confident in their status and good looks. Early on I'd tried a couple of passes at Dolly. She blew me off. And then when later that school year I'd told Carol about her, Carol had laughed so hard she got tears in her eyes. That hurt. Carol realized how harsh she'd been and hugged me. She added the observation that she'd briefly TA'd a class that Dolly was in and described her as a bubble-brained bitch, all fluff. I'd learned for myself about the bitch part, the airhead part was new. The pedestal I'd put her on shattered. I owed Carol for that. She was big on truth; painful consequences be damned. And a she could be a little arrogant, like me.

The culturally inappropriately monikered Pontiac and I galloped along at eighty-five miles per hour. In those days you could drive fifteen over and no one gave a damn, even at night and in the fog—which is what I was doing. U.S. Route 30 (the "0" meant it was a coast-to-coast road) ran practically door-to-door between Cicero and Mt. Vernon. My dad's Pontiac Star Chief was a classy, smooth ride. I felt like a million bucks. I say it was my dad's because he was very proud of the "Chief" even though he only drove for weekly bank runs or on the occasional mystery run with a bag full of cash. Mom drove most of the time, especially at night. I drove a bunch after I got my permit.

The car was a dark green two-tone, accented by a white hood top and white front fenders. The first thing that caught the eye was the massive, delta-winged hood ornament. It was bracketed by two strips of chrome that, like racing stripes, ran the length of the hood. Matching trim bracketed squarish tail fins. Below the gaping radiator intake and in line with the hood strips were two ram-jet nose-coned cylinders that protruded like defiant breasts of a chrome-nippled dominatrix.

I was one with the car, infused with the air rushing through the intakes, the cyclic throbbing of the internal combustion engine, and the hot gases escaping through the twin rocket tailpipes. The white-walled tires and fender skirt over the rear wheel-well topped off the machine's transmogrification into a white-hoofed beast, hot-blooded and quick to rage.

A welcoming committee of zero awaited me. A disappointment, after all the effort I'd made to procure the beast. I grabbed pizza and took it back to the dorm. I figured Carol was staying with Cyrus, so I hit the sack, the sack being my own bed.

When the two of us were there, I slept in a sleeping bag on the floor between the bed and the window.

The lacy hem of her A-line sleeveless dress didn't get in the way as we danced. I imagined stepping on it and the whole thing tearing off just under the bodice, like a tear-to-open package. Colleagues in the English department graciously brushed aside her condition, asked her to dance and generally were, well, collegial. One woman asked me to dance. She was tipsy and enjoyed brushing her breasts against my arms. Professor DeBricke's wife was glued to his side, so he behaved.

"You look like a sunset surrounded by colored stars." I'd meant that as a compliment. Carol's dress was a pale orange. A thin, pale-green wool sweater with silver speckles draped over her bare shoulders.

We'd taken a break earlier that night to watch the neatly trimmed corn fields shimmer and then get tucked in by the dark. Moths and mosquitoes migrated through The Barn's opened doors and swarmed sagging strings of colored lights. The warm odor of livestock and cut hay thickened air already warm from bodies and top-hatted propane space-heaters.

She laughed, "I'll take it as a compliment. Better than looking like a pumpkin, which is what I feel like."

The band was good and as the night progressed the music grew louder and folks got drunker. We drank watered-down lemonade. Carol avoided sweet or caffeinated drinks. She said that if Shirley Temple hated Shirley Temples, so could she. I wasn't very good at the academic chit-chat and soldiered on like Carol's majordomo, but with no one to command. I wanted her to have a good time. She picked up on my mood.

"Allez, on y va," she brushed my ear with her lips. It tickled and made me tilt away from her and smile. "I want to show you something."

We made our farewells and good-byes. Carol did all the talking on the way out. I nodded and shook hands with people I'd recently met and whose names I'd already forgotten.

When we got to the car, I asked "Where to?" She had clothes stashed at Curtis's place and at the dorm. We didn't have a plan for after the dance. And we were mobile.

"Mono Pond. It's not far, a quarter mile. But I can't walk in these shoes."

We had no problem finding our green beast in the haybale-bordered parking lot. I led Carol by the arm and all gentleman-like held the door.

We arrived in ten minutes. The side road dead-ended in a copse of deciduous trees surrounding the cat-tailed still life that was Mono Pond. Crickets and katydids battled with Ludwig drums and Fender guitars banging away at the Barn. To the west sheet lightning hop-scotched across the welkin. A storm was building.

"This what you wanted to show me? It's real peaceful-like."

"Yes, but there's more." She paused and twisted her back toward me. "Unzip, please. I can't breathe."

I'm a doer. I am not an observer. Some people are watchers. They pick up on things. I just act. I undid a clasp at her neck and unzipped the back of her dress. Not a lot, maybe four or five inches.

"Better?" I asked.

"More. All the way, please."

I did as ordered, careful to not catch the fabric in the zipper.

"The bra. Undo the bra."

That must have been what was so tight. I'd hate wearing anything that tight around my chest.

"Can you breathe now?"

Carol answered by slipping off one shoulder strap, then the other and taking in a big breath. "Phew." The top of her dress fell forward. I put my hands on the wheel. She leaned back and slid under my arms and across my lap.

You'd think it would be cooler here, next to Mono Pond, and the weather coming in. The windshield started to fog up. I got the message. I mean, I kinda picked it up a while ago when we were dancing but blamed the lemonade or something for my slowness. She wanted to make out. I didn't know if college seniors were still into that sort of thing, but I guess so. I'd always found Carol attractive but, you know, we were friends and I didn't want to wreck that. I took my job seriously. I was her bodyguard and I was proud of my upstanding behavior. And, of course, elle était enceinte.

She took in another huge breath and sighed out loud, from the chest, like she was doing Yoga. Her breath smelled good. "Much better. Thank you, Otto."

I felt hesitant. Maybe, after all, I wasn't much of a doer and she didn't want to make out. My damp hands stayed on the wheel and I focused on the black silhouette of a dead tree. Just as matter-of-factly, Carol reached under her dress with both hands, loosed, and then shed both undies and pantyhose. "Too tight," she said and rolled over to hands and knees. She managed the act with unexpected ease, given that we were on the bench seat and the dress fanned out like a ballerina's tutu.

"*This* is what I wanted to show you."

She wasn't drunk and she wasn't kidding. Carol unbuttoned the top of my pants (no belt), unzipped the fly, took my cock in her mouth, and gave me a mind-blowing blow-job—my first. She used one hand for me and touched herself with the other. Sometimes she'd jiggle my penis across her nipples. I gripped the wheel tight as hell when we came. The whole business had taken only a couple of minutes.

She mumbled something and pointed to her mouth. "Can't talk," she said without closing her lips together.

We laughed and she spit cum all over my crotch and wiped her mouth with my underwear.

Carol had left a straw bag of sundries on the floor. She extracted a water bottle and took a swig. She mumbled something again and made the same hand signal as before. This time I got what she wanted. I fumbled with the keys and then the switch and lowered the window. She spit outside, rolled over, and lay with the back of her head in my lap, ignoring the mess it would make of her hair and perhaps unaware of how erotic the entanglement was for me. My hand settled on her breast. Carol lightly pressed my hand against her chest. It was like holding warm bread. I didn't want anything to change, not the peace I felt inside, not the quiet stirrings of life at Mono Pond. But—isn't there always a *but*—the more I tried to relax and the more I let the sounds and smells of sex and summer fill me, the more aroused I became. That happens to teenagers.

Carol broke the silence. She sat up and rubbed her forehead head against mine. "Let's fuck, Otto Pulaski." We drank some water like two fighters hydrating for the next round.

My first thought was that I didn't have any condoms. Not that I ever carried condoms with me. I'd practiced with one once and put the damn thing on backward.

"Sois-tranquil. It's not like I'm going to get pregnant."

"Can you? I mean when you're—"

Carol had anticipated the thought. "Let's find out, shall we!" The words came with a playful kiss.

"Move over," she ordered. I dutifully slid to the passenger's side. Carol got on hands and knees facing the driver's door, backing up to avoid being scrunched by the wheel. She pulled her dress up so it fanned out around her backside. Her buttocks and vagina were like the center of a giant tulle-petaled flower, some *objet d'art* de Georgia O'Keefe, silky smooth and hairless. Did women shave every day like men? Probably not, or Burma Shave would've figured it out and I would've seen signs. I guessed shaving was a premeditated act, something a woman—and maybe a man—did when she or he wanted to feel pretty and attractive. Well, Carol was that: pretty and attractive. And mind-numbingly hot.

"First time?"

"Not quite, but like this, yeah." I wasn't going to bullshit Carol. She was too good a friend. And too savvy—she was running the show.

"You sure you're okay? The best, you know, comes later. After sex."

I didn't know what that meant and didn't care. The windows had completely fogged. I was in a cloud. Maybe Carol, too.

We'd been at it for a while, rocking the Ponti and fogging the windows when the door-latch clicked. I froze. Carol was still grinding away. The door crept open like a casket in a horror flick. I peeked over the top of the tulle and stared straight into the lunatic eyes of Jock who-is-not-Jacques the lumberjack, the man with the perfect five-o'clock shadow, the man with the Yin-yang face, the man who, I immediately realized, was holding a double-barreled shot-gun and pointing it at Carol's head. The cool air from outside hit my nose and I sneezed.

"Bless . . . you. Shit." Carol's body stiffened. I flagged.

No gesundheit from Jock: "The Lord says you c'ain't 'ave that baby."

The twin barrels of the shotgun looked me in the eyes. Carol rose between us. Not that it would do much good but it was a defiant and damned brave act. I think a point-blank shot-gun blast would take off both our heads. Deux d'un coup.

I never panic. It's not in my DNA. At times I wished I could panic. But nope, when I'm in the middle of dying, I'll ride it out to the bitter end. I reached in the glove box, praying Dad had forgotten to remove the silver revolver before lending me the car. It was there. My fingers wrapped around the cold silver handle and found the trigger. I slipped my hand with the weapon under Carol's armpit, aimed blindly, and pulled the trigger. The round connected with something, but I couldn't see what.

I shoved Carol down and watched Jock stumble backward and trip. He hit the ground hard and the muzzle of the shotgun flashed. The stars shook, animals scattered in the brush, our ears rang.

I wrapped an arm under Carol and crawled atop her to see better. Jock was still moving. He rolled up to one elbow and tried to re-aim the weapon. I didn't hesitate and pulled the trigger a second time. I visualized putting down a rabid dog. Warm vomit from Carol ran over the back of my arm. Steam came off our bodies. Another flash—lightning this time—illuminated clouds closing in on Mono Pond. A second shot-gun blast ripped the sky a new one. A deluge commenced. That was creepy. I thought about the creepiness, the timing of it, and wondered if I'd forever have freakish fears of alcoholic mothers or mental lovers whenever I had sex. My pecker curled up like a fiddlehead fern.

Jock rose out of the muck like he was auditioning for *The Creature from the Black Lagoon*. No shotgun this time. He hobbled away from us and vanished in the black void. I didn't care if he was shot, not then. I care now and tell myself he was walking so he was alive when we left him. Carol hugged her sweater and wiped vomit from her mouth. I yanked up my pants and returned the warm gun to the glovebox. We swapped places and drove off.

Torrential rain dogged us all the way to Curtis's trailer in Iowa city. Every few minutes, silhouettes of barns, trees, and hills were illuminated and extinguished. We jumped when we passed a State Trooper patrol car on the side of the road and splattering red and blue light on the aluminum, ribbed siding of dead semi-trailer. We drove without speaking, letting the rain speak for us. Whatever was going to happen tomorrow could wait until tomorrow.

At Curtis's, Carol and I showered, got naked, and shared the bed. The revolver had burned and bruised her under-arm and armpit, but we were too exhausted to administer first aid. She fell asleep instantly. I was up the entire night, holding her and thinking, and half-expecting officer Iona to knock at the door. Or Jock. I hoped to hell I hadn't killed him. The gun was under the pillow. The odor of gunpowder residue mixed with the perfume the shower had failed to wash away.

Who I was and who I would become—all of it—had been reset.

My hands spread across her swollen belly. I felt its irregular contour and its dimension, how it fit under the expanse of my hand. I felt or imagined I felt the stirrings of her child. *Jock is dead, long live Jock* played in my head. As did Carol's comment, about the best being later. Was this the "later"? The two of us snuggled up and in this deep, strong, and enduring closeness. She was right.

Rain and hail hammered the tinny roof and walls. Carol slept. Wind snatched at the flimsy door. Carol slept. My thoughts rode the storm's violent tide, keenly aware of its apposition to the physical tranquility within my hands. Carol, la femme enceinte, slept.

Amant: / a.mã / noun / lover (masc.)

Zoom 7

"I heard you changed your name," I said. I wanted a conversation redirect. The rest of the family, the ones still on the call, surely wanted the same.

"Thinking about it," Zadie said.

Mom parachuted in. "She's not really changing her name, Otto. It's a harmless exploration. Teenagers do that all the time."

"Lay it on me. What's the new one!"

"Zack."

"Like Zacharia or Isaac?"

"Um, dunno. They're both Hebrew?"

"I think so," I said, though not sure. "I like Zack with an 'h' or a 'k'." I was genuinely enthusiastic. "I like snappy names."

"You call me Zades. Zack is like that."

"Nice ring to it—Zack Pulaski. Got punch. Like you, Zades."

"Yeah, 'I'm a Pulaski, just ask me!' Remember that?" Zadie exclaimed.

Mom choppered in. "That's not a very feminine name, dear. What's wrong with Zadie?"

"You know, Kali, in some cultures, adolescents chose a new name when they're Zadie's age."

"Not this one," she rifled back.

"Well," I said, "how about I change my name? A grandpa bonding thing."

I had wanted to shift the conversation away from me and realized after the fact that I had just done a U-turn. Plus, I sounded like I wanted to be Zadie's pal or buddy. I don't. I believe that families are and should be hierarchies.

"Cool!" said my enthusiastic granddaughter.

Kali reengaged, sensing an opportunity to say something nasty. "Your Papa Otto has had a number of nicknames."

Seemed like I wasn't the only one hitting the sauce. Kali's not a happy drunk, she's a mean one. Though not as vicious as her mom, Eluine, who was in a class of her own and had a deeply honest meanness, a meanness that bordered on the sublime.

"Such as?" Zadie asked.

I didn't say a word. After an uncomfortable silence that conveyed my clear reluctance to go down this path, Kali took point.

"An Army buddy called him Potto. Your Papa Otto was a hippy, a war protester." That was humiliating but true. One thing Army guys and war protesters had in common was smoking shitloads of weed. I did protest against the war. More than just protest, actually.

"Is that true, Papa Otto? I didn't know. Were you in Vietnam?"

"Here's a puzzle, Zadie. Rearrange the letters in my name and you'll—"

Zadie, quick as a Jeopardy vet, slapped the 'I got the answer' button. "Toot!"

"Bingo! Tooter." Tooter's what a few ex-friends called me.

"Tooter's cute!" Zadie laughed. "Can I call you Papa Tooter?"

"Please don't."

"Was Vietnam awful? Mom said—"

"Just kids, camping in tents and reading The Jungle Book. What do I know . . ."

Kali knew the land mines and stonewalling to come. "Don't bother, Zadie. You won't get a straight answer."

Someone from the peanut gallery opined. "Damned pacifist . . ."

"You don't like talk about it, do you?" Zadie was more than just academic smart. I said nothing as she responded to her own question. "No biggie."

Kali, knowing it or not, gave the knife a twist. "Those names embarrass him, Zadie. And you'll be embarrassed if you decide to call yourself Zack!"

She's right, of course, at least about me. Embarrassment and shame often go hand-in-hand with doing the right thing. She's right about everything. Is that what distanced us? She was born knowing what's right and I had to beat myself up to get to the same place. Not even the same place, but some hackneyed version of it.

"Ceteris paribus," Zadie unloaded the Latin. "It's a different time, you know. Like it was a very different time way back then. And Papa Otto is right. That war was stupid." The words trembled with

anger. I hadn't expected the emotional connection and thought about Mlle Lachenal. "All wars are stupid."

A quiet beat passed. Were they waiting for a Zadie meltdown or an angry outburst from me? It felt like Zadie had the floor and that no one, not even the Mom, had the courage to challenge her.

"I believe," Zadie stated — it was a recovery move, "that Vietnam was once a French colony. Indochina. That's what it was called."

She was suddenly the adult in the virtual room and speaking in a voice that conveyed a regained composure and an icy edge.

This time, I was grateful to be drifting back to le français territory.

"Indochine." I offered up the French name, wishful that Zadie and I could find safety by speaking in French. I knew a little about Southeast Asia. And I knew that any political conversation would spiral out of control.

"Have you read L'Amant?" I asked. "By Maguerite Duras?"

Kali groaned, a little too loudly, a "tell" that showed either frustration or relief that Zadie and I had moved on. "That's not appropriate reading for a girl her age, Otto." She took a deep breath and continued in the same pedantic tone. "You know, you don't say the last letter of any French word unless it's C, R, F or L. Like in CaReFuL." She did this funny thing spreading her fingers for the capital letters and squeezing them into little fists for the small ones.

I didn't correct her correction. Duras was the name the author had chosen as a pen name. It's the name of the town in France where her father was from. The 's' is pronounced.

I took my turn at pedantry: "Duras was born and grew up in Saigon. L'Amant — the Lover, in English — is a semi-autobiographical tale about a love affair that a fifteen-year-old girl has with a wealthy

Chinese man. The story, especially in French, is beautiful. It's distant and abstract—hard to pull off in English, the distancing."

One's adult children, once they've staked out their place in the world, can be damned judgmental. Kali, no exception to the rule, dug in her heels: "And it was rape. Don't dress it up, Otto. Bad influence. Bad, bad, bad."

"Have you read it?" I asked Kali.

"Saw the movie. That was enough."

"The movie is about sex. The book isn't. It's misunderstood, like Lolita is misunderstood."

"More rape," Kali said. "Jesus, Otto."

Zadie was curious. You could tell she was taking mental notes. I expected a segue on the rape topic but that's not what followed.

"What bad-for-you books did you read when you were my age?"

"The Razor's Edge, by Somerset Maugham."

"At Cornell?"

"Yes, Cornell. The story is about a man who chose experiential knowledge over academic. It's been so long. I'm sure I'm misremembering. That book gave me the excuse I'd been looking for. After flunking out, me and my Homer hit the road."

"There you have it," Kali added. "Bad book, ergo," she stressed the Latin word, "bad choices."

"Did Duras"—Zadie pronounced the author's name with the 's' at the end—"have a real affair, or is it all made-up?"

"I don't know. The book is semi-autobiographical. The story is set near Saigon. The girl in the story is unnamed. To read L'Amant is . . ." I hunted for words. "It's like breathing in the foreign and familiar, being suspended between generations, between cultures, between being a girl and a woman, between being a victim and a predator. Duras made no reference to the Vietnam of today. And I think she never gave a name to the protagonist. That's one thing that makes the story dream-like, like you're afloat in the author's memory. And the use of the present tense—makes the story immediate, sot of timeless."

"The author," Kali commented, "she was adrift alright. I read she was drunk when she wrote L'Amant. The woman was an alcoholic and the book is an obscene rant."

Do I shut up? What the hell! "Rape, sure. But also a power struggle. We cheer for the underdog, hope for fairness or justice. We respond to whatever button Duras pushes in us because the story is so sparse that we have to fill in the empty parts with our own biases and preconceptions. There's no crutch, no Raskolnikov or Lucrece through whom the writer exposes the pros and cons of the characters' actions and feelings. In the end, good or bad, the affair in L'Amant is intimate and about power and identity. Though an unfair fight, the combatants ravage each other for what they need."

All coming-of-age experiences run their course and as adults we sanitize and rebrand the narrative. We repeat our precious fabrications until we believe them. I thought about Jock, poor Jock. When you maybe kill someone, it doesn't mean that you've suddenly become a master of your own fate. Nor when you experience sex, is it the case that sex is now something you understand. Both are a quantum leap in experience, but not maturity. In our teens, even well into our twenties, we still haven't biologically matured—neither bodies nor minds. Young women and young men can appear malleable and fearless, their visions of the world fueled by those who hold sway over underdeveloped expectations and values. There is a segment of young people who refuse to yield and insist, whatever the cost, on finding their own way. I wondered at the imagined maturity and ferocity of the *young Duras—was it wishful thinking on the author's part or self-aware fearlessness in the living, real protagonist?*

I was aware of this while speaking with Zadie. And aware that whatever her choices would be, I didn't want her to go through what I had gone through when, at an equally vulnerable age, if not precisely in years but in sensibility, I was compelled, threatened, or lured into performing acts wherein I was incapable of responsible consent.

Indochine

Only once did I talk about the war and the shaming and courage it entailed. I was in Washington D. C. at a victory celebration and conference put on by a Colorado Congressman I'd supported. I'm not politically inclined but I had made an exception this time because I'd had first-hand knowledge that my Congressman's opponent was a crook. I didn't want a shady crook representing my district in Congress. I was thirty and an up-and-coming venture capital associate, too naïve and too full of myself to appreciate how widespread and insidious the corruption in Washington was, nor how intractably stacked the deck was—and still is—against justice and democracy and the poor.

But back to my story. I had finished dinner with several boring election co-workers at one of those D. C. Brazilian churrascaria restaurants where waiters serve unconscionable quantities of meat to patrons aspiring to hypercholesterolemia. I'd had a few, and although it was after midnight I'd opted to return to my hotel on foot and sober up in the cool spring air.

En route, while walking under a row of elms that blocked light from streetlights, I saw a man hidden by the shadows and dragging a woman up the steps to the front door of a nondescript brownstone. I stopped to let my eyes adjust to the dark. One of her pumps fell off and the man reached down, grabbed the shoe, and stuffed it in his pocket.

I crept up the steps. Her feet disappeared through the doorway and into an impossibly dark hallway. I charged in.

As the assailant was dragging her, she spoke: "Aide-moi . . . je me sens mal . . ." It was a whisper but I caught enough to know she must be hurting.

I confronted him and took hold of the padded shoulder and back of his suit coat and yanked him away from her. Underneath the padding, I felt his muscles tense and then relax.

"What the fuck's going on . . ." I threatened.

"Gimme a hand," he ordered. The words were slurred.

The woman groaned, "Am I home?" The English was slightly accented.

"You're home, dearie. How you doing?" the assailant asked.

"Tummy's not so good. My feet are killing me. Merci." She rested herself on her elbows. "Dark as shit in here."

She saw me and started. "Who the fuck is he!"

The man I had thought was her assailant stayed cool. "He helped me. You're a big girl, you know."

"I don't know if that's a nice thing to say or not." She burped unceremoniously. "Nice of you to help, mister whoever you are." There was a lull before she burped again. This time it smelled like throw-up. "Gentlemen, a lady's gotta go stick her head in the toilet. You boys," she shooed us away, "party on . . ."

Further assurances and farewells followed. The man put the shoe on the floor. He took my arm. We leaned on each other and clumsily descended the stairs.

"Fucking bold, creeping up on me. Complete fuck-with-my-head surprise."

"That was the idea, sorry. I couldn't see for shit," I said, "you know, wanted to make sure she was okay."

"Yeah, she is A.O.K." He punched out the letters. "C'mon."

I followed and we ended up at a nearby bar.

"You're lucky The Colonel didn't fucking kill you," someone said. "Comin' up on 'im from behind like that."

They were all smashed, maybe a dozen people, no women. I forget the reason for the celebration, but it had something to do with the Disabled Vietnam Veterans lobby. They didn't look disabled. Maybe dysfunctional. The more we drank, the more they talked and the more I learned. One guy, a very fit black dude, didn't say a word. In my head I called him Quiet Guy.

"He can kill you in a second, man, you know that?" someone else, a guy with a cane, said, referring again to The Colonel. "Tell him!"

The Colonel, demurred. "Never been in a fight."

"Right," the same someone snarled and followed up with a tale about The Colonel's escape from a prison in North Vietnam and his solo, month-long, trek back to the south along the Ho Chi Minh trail. Later that night, The Colonel clarified his earlier statement about never having been in a fight. Apparently, he could kill someone in seconds—and had done so—but he had never been in a fisticuffs bar fight.

Story followed story. Army guys love and need their stories. By three a.m. the waiters' eyes showed the wear and tear of the night. The staff wanted us out so they could go home and go to bed.

My tablemates were insisting I tell my story. I declined but said what I thought. "I hated the war. Maybe it was the right war, and at the right time, but we were on the wrong side. I was too young to know anything more than that I didn't trust the people telling me what to do."

That didn't go over as poorly as I'd expected, at least for the first sixty seconds. The lout sitting next me, nothing disabled about him that I could see, downed his whiskey and grabbed my arm. "Talk, hippie." I didn't look like a hippie. I was a poster child for Armani and Bally. To these guys, though, I suddenly became The Hippie.

The bill had been paid. Except for our group, the restaurant was empty. Lout's threat signaled to the staff that the time had come to shoo us out the door. Our numbers were down to four, not counting me: Quiet Guy, The Colonel, someone I had yet to tag, and Lout.

"This way," one of them said and led our pack across the street and along a darkened path through some park I don't remember the name of.

We stopped at a small clearing. Lout was behind me and grabbed the shoulders of my suit jacket and roughly yanked them down and across my upper arms. It's a maneuver I knew, one that's used to stabilize a captured combatant. He whipped out his belt and cinched my hands behind my back. By the book, so far. The Colonel watched as I stood silent. I was pissed to high heaven but not so pissed that I didn't know that I was being prepped for prisoner interrogation. Lout knocked the back of my knees and I went to the ground. My knees sank into the wet sod.

One of them took hold of my tie and tightened it around my throat and lifted upward. My head lolled to the side, like the head of someone being hanged. I said nothing, did nothing. I was too drunk to fight. In these situations, you want to appear as compliant as possible. Until you're not. I wasn't engaged but I was aware of everything in my immediate surroundings. Duras would have called it a state of *expenditure.* Empty and silent, French silent, where it's a self-reflective *act* to make oneself be silent, se taire.

"You gonna talk now?" I stared at a gap in the man's teeth and noted the odor of tequila, cheap tequila with a plastic worm in the bottle.

"There's a worm in your mouth," I said. That's when I tagged him 'Worm.'

He whacked me across the face. "Talk, you fucking hippie shit."

"Sure." I hoped that if I said something he'd loosen the grip on my tie. It's hell to talk when you're being strangled. "Hated the war and paid my dues. You know, I'm over it, and you, you dumb fuck, it's gotcha by the balls."

I wasn't afraid. Not that this confrontation was fun; I'm not that kind of arrogant. I'd been afraid before and what was happening right now did bring back memories of being in a stockade cell and threatened by a crazed meth-head guard with big, dilated pupils.

That beating never happened. My cellie, a kid from Okinawa, had my back. He was there because he had cleaned out a bar and sent five guys to the infirmary. He told the guard to fuck off or he would kill him. He didn't raise his voice. He didn't get out of his bunk. We got along, Cellie and me. He stood up for me. I think because I was always straight with him, and respectful. Respect goes a long way.

You might wonder now, What does scare the shit out of Otto? Plenty. It's making the decision that you'd rather die or kill yourself than murder a bunch of innocent people. It's acting less on knowledge and mostly on a gut feeling that a fucking war was not about rights or justice, but about a handful of greedy, fucking politicians and corporations that wanted ever more power and money and that your life and lives of hapless others were their means to get it. It's making a decision that is an existential antidote to our capacity to do violence to one another for little or no good reason.

"Fuck you." Someone said. It was hard *fuck you*, not a 'hey, you took my parking space' fuck you.

"You want to know what I did?" I was angry. "I helped hopeless dumb fucks like you have a chance, go to Canada and get a new dumb-fuck life. Think about it, asshole," I didn't raise my voice, "and get your head outta the shitter."

After that exchange, Lout and Worm roughed me up a little. Was this a *mock* interrogation? The tie, my favorite Armani tie, tightened around my neck. I cared about the tie and didn't want to get blood on it.

Being drunk makes me philosophical. Always has. What the fuck, I mused. Another notch for Darwin, a harmless spider washed down the drain, an idealist strangled in the park by a madman with PTSD—it was all the same senseless shit to me. I'm One with the cherry blossoms and a pawn in the endless cycle of life, death, and—cross you fingers—rebirth. I cheerfully inhaled the odor of cherry blossoms . . . And smiled.

Quiet Guy raised a hand; they stopped fucking with me.

"How 'bout I tell ya *my* story," Quiet Guy said. "Third tour, we was patrolin' some butt-fuck nowhere village perimeter 'n we got this curfew 'n anybody out after curfew we shoot. Every 'body' counted." He put "body" in air quotes. "Fuckin' war by the fuckin' numbers. So we shoot anythin' makes the number bigger: women, old men, little kids, water fuckin' buffalo, dogs. Don't. Fuckin'. Matter." He took a breath and scanned the men, making eye contact with each man in turn. "We 'spect 'em after we shoot 'em. Verification, ya see. There's this old woman. Fuckin' musta been sixty if she's a day. She meant no harm an' I put two neat little holes right through her frail little heart; 'bout inch apart. 'Nice group' says my spotter. Then he makes this weird face." Quiet Guy imitated the spotter's face, nodding his head, corners of the mouth turned down, and sticking out his lower lip like he'd just had a spoonful of soup and thought it tasted pretty damned good. "I fucked him up good."

"How *fucked* is that?" Quiet Guy paused here. Nobody had the balls to interrupt to ask if he had meant shooting the old woman or fucking up the spotter. Quiet Guy let the hurt inside go from boil to simmer.

He spat and continued, "I'll tell ya."

He had our attention, I'll tell ya. "I figur'd out right then 'n there. Had an epi-finity. Threw my goddamned rifle on the ground 'n never touched the fuckin' thing agin. Didn't say shit. Didn't say shit for a year. Not one mother-fuckin' word. Figur'd if I said one word and somebody said somethin' back to me I'd kill 'em 'n I was done w' killing.

" 'ventually some brass asshole flipped a coin. Heads the nuthouse, tails Leavenworth. They gave me a fuckin' medal, you know that? For *what!*" Droplets of spit flew from his mouth, angry tears filled his eyes. "Like I give a fuck about a goddamn tin-shit medal." Quiet Guy's voice drifted off. I could just make out the words. "Lord Jesus Christ Almighty, forgive me fer I have really fuckin' sinned."

Quiet Guy settled somewhat. He pointed at me. "This here fuckin' hippie," he paused. " he got cojones to go up them steps 'n help a woman what he don't know. Tunnel rat dark, ya know, 'n kinda dumb. 'specially 'cause The Colonel be there." Quiet Guy pointed at The Colonel. "Respec' that. He did what he figur'd right. The sonna bitch problie did what he figur'd right way back when. Ya understan' me fuck-heads?"

They heard good. Worm loosened the knot against my throat. Lout un-cinched the belt around my wrists.

"Trade ya, Hippie." Quiet Guy took off his tie and handed it to me. Then he helped me up. I said good-bye to my favorite Armani. "Don't fergit."

I never forgot. When I look back on it, not this incident in the park but my little tiff with the Army, I always have second thoughts. Always. Did I do the right thing? I accept duty. I'm respectful of the military and the military was always square with me. Before they handed over that DD-214 they offered to hook me up with some fancy intelligence job. Pick an MOS, pick a language, tell us where you want to go. We need smart people like you, especially ones with language skills. Was it philosophical integrity (that's what I told myself at the time), honor, fear of letting down my draft resistance cohorts, fear of abetting moral wrong-doing, fear of releasing that goddamn violence lurking in a dark corner of my soul and eager to ratchet up the kill count? I don't know what it was, but something made me say no. Or maybe it was simply love, my first real love, for a woman I didn't truly know but who had begun to take up so much space in my heart and eventually became my wife.

So, what was Vietnam to me? It was a story whose significance lies in its not being told. A story that, like *L'Amant,* could be wishful thinking or fearlessness, a story about power and violence, and a story that is most certainly missing names.

Rêverie: / ʁɛ.vʁi / noun / daydream

Zoom 8

The text was a shocker.

<<ZP: Can we meet? Like in person?>>

<<OP: Not so easy.>>

<<ZP: Why not?>>

<<OP: Your mom would flip. And you are there and I am here.>>

<<ZP: You love your granddaughter?>>

<<OP: Yes, but she's a pain in the butt. You okay Zades?>>

<<ZP: How would you know! You're like banished and we never hang.>>

I worried for a minute that she might take my reaction the wrong way so I texted a few hearts. She responded in kind.

<<OP: I'm a sketchy guy. We shouldn't text.>>

<<ZP: Says who?>>

Kali noticed Zadie with eyes down, obviously focused on the phone and not her computer's camera, and followed up with a predictable parental muttering, "Teenagers." The few folks who remained on the call tried to outdo each other with tales about phones dropped in toilets, rear-end collisions by texters, texts going to the wrong people—those were the most common. I'm a careful guy. I'd never screw up like that.

<<ZP: You mean you're not perfect? Me too. I do bad stuff. Ask Mom. No don't. But you're not a child molester or rapist, are you? Nothing creepy?>>

<<OP: Jesus, Zades. No!>>

Oddly, it was Kali who brought up the subject of French again. Earl's sister was planning a post-COVID Mediterranean cruise with a stop in France. If it were up to me I'd torpedo the goddamn cruise ships. They made Nice uninhabitable. And had destroyed Venice. Ask Donna Leon. She had to move to Switzerland.

"Otto, where was that place in France you went to that you said was so quiet? Center something. I don't remember."

"Yeah. I remember the place, but I don't remember where it was. I mean I was just driving around, reached a dead end of a dirt road. I stayed only a few days."

"What did you call it, again?"

That I remembered well: "Le Centre du Silence."

Zadie added another question. "You were grown up then. Were you living in France?"

"Working there, off and on."

<<SP: Oo-la-la. Working on what, Papa Otto? Another crush!!>> Zadie texted.

I laughed and did exactly what I'd just told myself I didn't do. I answered out loud, "No, no crushes."

Kali picked up the non sequitur. "What? What did you say?"

"No crashes," I said, making a slick recovery. "But my car broke down. Stayed at some old house there. Only French speakers. It was a good cultural experience. They called a mechanic, and he fixed the car. I left."

<<ZP: Good save, Papa Otto! We're going to meet. I don't care what Mom says. Or the stupid lawyers. Are there lawyers? I'm a bad girl and I like it.>>

"Shit," I fucked up a second time and got inquisitive gawks from the chicken heads bobbling on the computer screen.

"Otto," someone said. I couldn't tell who. "You crashed?!"

That person cared, whoever it was. Or maybe it was morbid curiosity. I played back the voice and put a name to the face. Earl's sister. Kali once told me that the sister reads the paper every day. The crime reports and the obits. Nothing else. Still, that was nice of her.

"Sorry," I lobbied for time. "Back in a minute. Teapot on the stove." I had to piss.

"You hate tea." Kali spiked the lie. Why not let it go? Is it pride?

"People change, Kali. Been watching **The Crown,** you know. They're always drinking tea." In for a penny, in for a pound. The thought deserved a groan.

"Don't watch the Sopranos, please," she retorted.

I didn't and I wouldn't. I don't like violence—in me or anyone. The thought brought me back to the side conversation with Zadie. I muted sound and switched off video, sitting on the can so I could still text.

<<OP: Z, there's not one molecule of you that's bad!>>

<<ZP: I didn't say bad person. I said bad girl, like in being a girl.>>

I had missed that. Flew right by, following a flight plan ordained by my preconceptions.

<<OP: Hey, be nice to yourself. What's going on?>> I was paying attention.

<<ZP: I want to be a boy. I feel like a boy. And I like girls. Does that make me gay, too? Or am I not gay if I think I'm a boy?>>

I was at sea as much as Zadie and afraid that my advice would, upon reflection, be banal or, even worse, damaging. <<OP: I dunno Z, just be you.>>

<<ZP: Yeah, tell Mom—>>

<<OP: Happy to—>>

<<ZP: Fuck don't!! Sorry, Papa Otto. Please don't. She knows. Sort of. What do you do?>>

Was that a rhetorical question? Or was the question literal? I answered as if I were the addressee.

<<OP: Moi? Je me promène.>>

I walk.

Le Centre du Silence

Le Centre de Silence. The name is worthy of capitalization. The magic of the place lies in its contrast to the events that had preceded my arrival there.

I had been raising money for a Colorado venture capital company. A significant chunk of the life of a venture capitalist is hustling money. VCs do it any way they can, usually starting with friends and relatives. When that tranche of money is tapped out, VCs branch out to investors who might have some strategic connection with the VC's portfolio companies. Eventually, and if the VC firm is successful and has a couple of Roman numerals after its upcoming fund, they hustle institutional money from pension funds, insurance companies, and big banks. The total amount of money this last group hands over to VCs might sound big, but it's a pittance compared to the total assets the group manages—which is many, many trillions. My company's targets in Switzerland were a handful of small, private banks. These were banks without agents or affiliates in the States, but with an interest in boarding the U.S. tech juggernaut.

Getting in the door was the hard part. The firm I worked with had just enough history to open exactly three doors in Zürich and two in Genève. On the side, I was working a possible merger between two rope/cord manufacturers: one in the U.S., Atlanta, to be precise, and the second in Viennes, France. Both were superbly managed family businesses.

The Zürich meetings were the day after I landed from NYC and they were back-to-back. The bankers were polite, and I was jet-lagged. We went through the motions. If I'd known then what I know now, I wouldn't have even tried to raise funds in Zürich. You have to have a local in, even if it's the banker's second cousin who's a farmer. I don't mean to denigrate Swiss farmers, Bauern in die Schweiz tend to be well-educated.

Later in life, I lived in Zürich; it's become my favorite city. Now I know how one connects. Importantly, it has nothing to do with wanting anything from anybody.

Let's say you're at someone's home for a Swiss National Day dinner. The day celebrates the alliance in 1291 of the three cantons of Uri, Schwyz, and Unterwalden. Initially, your hosts and other guests politely speak English. Today, English is the second language for almost everyone in Switzerland. This is true regardless of one's first language, typically a dialect of one of the four official languages: German, French, Italian, and Romansch. Even in Romansch country, with less than fifty-thousand speakers and where the language varies significantly from one village to the next, the locals speak some English. In Zürich, after a few beers or glasses of wine, the partiers begin to relax and drift into the high German. That's still being polite. If you've had any German training, it's relatively easy going. But when the group warms up, eau de vie poire hour, the old folks start telling tales. The talk slips into the local dialect of Swiss German and everybody's too lit to care about translating. You're family now. Talk's less polite and you sink or swim. People slap you on the back and revel in your confusion about what the hell everybody is laughing at. I love Swiss German and wear my irreparably corrupted Hochdeutsch like a badge of honor.

Not knowing the local lingo, the money dance in Zürich went nowhere. Discouraged but hopeful that I'd have better luck in Genève, I hit the road. Sleep-deprived and made sleepier still by a baking, hot afternoon sun, I pulled over at Chateau d'Œx and booked a room at a chalet-like inn advertising a restaurant with local cuisine. The d'Œx is pronounced like 'day.' A lot easier to say than it looks.

Chateau d'Œx is a small burg in the French-speaking Vaud canton. It's in the Pays-d'Enhaut, which I guess you would roughly translate as *high country*, and is a ski town in the winter and hiking and ballooning center in the summer.

Subscribing to some hocus-pocus about exercise being a way of exorcising jet lag, I dumped my bag in my room, slipped into a tee, Adidas running shorts and shoes, slurped a little water from the sink faucet, and headed out the door. Across the street a path led to a local summit about six kilometers or so from the trailhead. It might have been Point de Cray, I don't remember the name. I do remember wet rock ridges and foothills with folds like green flesh and drying in the sunlight. And I remember sweating—a lot of sweating—and regretting that I had brought no water.

Somewhere along the path, I lost the trail and began cutting across squared off meadows with waist-high grass and alpine flowers. Barbed wire fencing separated the fields. I had to carefully press down the wire to step over it. The fields were a minefield of muck and manure. Near the top of the ridge and while stepping over a fence, I slipped. A razor barb snagged the fleshy part of my calf. Blood spurted out and I had to lay in the grass, raised the leg, and keep pressure on the wound. After a few minutes, the bleeding subsided. My objective—the top of ridge—was a few hundred meters away. There, a plump, foliaged tree shaded a bench from which one could scan the panorama to the south. I approached and made out the figure of a hunchbacked man, sitting and with his hands stacked atop a walking stick braced between his legs. Given his age and condition, he must have ridden the cable car and traversed the path along the ridge to the overlook.

The man was overdressed: a faded beret, long pants, sturdy shoes, and a wool coat too long and too warm for the day but nevertheless buttoned to the neck. An undertaker, a bundle of bones, that was my first impression. The man didn't turn his head to greet me, though he surely had seen me ascending from below.

I needed to rest before the descent. I'd have to walk or jog as I had no money for the téléphérique. The man's body bounced when I plopped down on the bench.

"Pardon," I said. "Ça vous dérange?"

"Pas du tout." he greeted me with a half-smile.

After several minutes of silence, during which time I had raised my leg and put it over the side of the bench to give the wound time to clot, he spoke. In French again, he commented about the fil barbelé, the barbed wire, and mentioned that he too had been ensnared and his body scarred by barbed wire. I didn't understand exactly what he had said, but I think he joked that the barbed wire in the war was less odious than that used by Swiss farmers. I asked about the war. This was WWII we were talking about. He said he had been in Belgium, and added very proudly that for a time he commanded a group that had been part of the Résistance Belge. He had lost many friends, he said, but his group had exacted vengeance. The Légion Belge had successfully assassinated Nazi commanders and local collaborateurs or, as he called them, "collaboos."

His words were Gauloise flavored whispers. He leaned into me when he spoke. Our faces almost touched. The whites of his eyes had yellowed; the irises, once perhaps a sapphire blue, seemed sapped of pigment. I asked if he lived here. He nodded yes and said it was for the health care, but that after the war he had been wounded and lived in France with a woman—"ma fleur de Lily"—who had been in the French resistance and who had cared for him at a place far from the fighting, far from anywhere. His description of the place was compelling and I was drawn into his reveries. I wondered if he'd made up the story. And then I wondered if I was really here, sitting on this bench, watching the shadows lengthen and listening to their tales as much as his.

I needed to return to my lodging before dark and faced a six-kilometer descent. My bench mate read my intention. He seemed a naturally patient and inquisitive man, someone who takes the time to assess in advance what others are thinking. As I rose, he surprised me by speaking English.

"My name is Albert Renard-Maes. I've enjoyed our conversation. Your French is coming along, you must continue to speak French at every opportunity."

We shook hands rather formally. I introduced myself. We both examined the gash on my leg.

"The bleeding has stopped," he assured me, then regained the position in which I had first found him. His gaze stretched to the glacier faceted peaks to the southwest, toward France and toward whatever reflections he had paused on my account.

Though seeping blood and dehydrated, I managed to stay on the path and make good time on the descent. The crowd at the restaurant through which I would have to pass to get to my accommodations was—given the early hour—surprisingly lively.

I opened the door, took two or three steps in, and was set upon by a server and a customer. A quiet expectation replaced the table talk and tinkling tableware.

A young server, probably a daughter of the owners, used the familiar form of address. "Tu es blessé!"

I didn't respond. She asked again, this time in English. I had understood the question but I was slow to form the words for a response in French.

"Wounded! No. I'm fine, thanks. I'm very thirsty. J'ai soif."

She retrieved a glass of water from a tray on the counter and handed it to me. I dispatched it in a single, long, satisfying drink. I noticed then, when the glass was still up by my face, that my hand was covered with dried blood. I lowered the glass and turned toward the mirror behind the bar. The face of a madman stared back at me. Wild strands of hair poked every which way; sweat had traced white, worm-like paths across a face covered in a gesso of dirt and blood.

"I'm sorry," I said and showed her the gash in my calf. "I need to wash."

She took my arm and walked me through the dining area and up the stairs to my room. I was grateful for the help and warmed from the way she clung to my arm. I thanked her at the door. She wiped her hands on her apron and immediately realized she would need to get a fresh apron. I smiled an I'm sorry. She returned the smile, did an about-face, and exited the room.

I guzzled the contents of a water bottle the staff had left on the sideboard and then went to the bathroom to clean up. That same frightening visage filled the mirror. Certainly, Albert Renard-Maes had noticed. And just as certainly, he had seen worse.

Genève went about as well as Zürich. I'd booked a room in Geneva's Old Town, the Vieille Ville, at Hôtel les Amures. The seventeenth-century structure had yet to be sugarcoated with the trappings of a wannabe five-star hotel. The place had character. I stayed in a tiny room on the top floor. I'm a little over six feet and beams across the ceiling were at five feet and change, meaning I cracked my skull against them when I got up at night to find the bathroom. The head bruises complemented nicks and scrapes from my run and all-in-all gave me a fresh-from-a-bar-fight aspect. The room wasn't cheap, but the concierge sold me on it when he said that Lenin used to stay that very room. I've since researched this claim and although it is true that Lenin spent time in Geneva, the concierge was blowing smoke.

My blitz through Europe had one more stop, Viennes, France. Determined to leave Lenin's room to Lenin's ghost, I wrapped up meetings and hit the road at six p.m., arriving in Viennes at eight, just in time to catch my business contact there in the middle of some celebratory event. I never figured out what the event was, but they called it an *accueil*, an impossible-to-pronounce French word that means something like "host" or "welcome." The welcoming wasn't for me but for my associate, who was charming and sociable, and prioritized partying over anything I'd come to discuss. To be polite, I joined the party. Not a word of English was spoken and after too much talk and too much wine, I made my adieu. Fresh blood stained my pant leg. Too sore and tipsy to walk, I drove—a good choice because I couldn't find the hotel that a now certifiably unreliable guest had recommended. In fact I couldn't find any hotel that was open. Finally, I noticed a tobacconist's shop that still had the lights on. It was well after midnight. When I asked about une chambre économique, the proprietor said nothing but rummaged around a desk drawer until he found a set of keys. He indicated that I follow him.

I prepaid in cash. The charge was less than a cheap bottle of wine. We felt our way up an unlit staircase reeking of urine. The sticky treads licked at the soles of my shoes. He showed me to a room with a cot for a bed and low sink with a dirty glass. A bare bulb swung from its cord and filled the air a thick, stale yellow light. A plywood sheet covered the only window. I forgot to ask about a bathroom. I pissed in the sink, left my clothes on to discourage bed bugs, and crashed for the night.

I awoke from a dream about a sledgehammer repeatedly whacking me in the head. The bed shook, the floor shook, the entire room shook. The thuds in my mental world merged into shudders in the physical world. I felt like shit. My head ached— fuck you, Lenin; fuck you, wine. The pounding intensified, as did the odors of urine and my smelly clothes. Blood had oozed out my half-bandaged calf, soaked through my pants, and congealed atop the bedspread. I could feel filth crawling around and under me and eager for my flesh.

The new day framed the plywood over the window. I drank a glass of brownish water, pissed in the sink again, grabbed my few things, and descended the now familiar and still sticky steps. Once outside, I saw it . . . An evil wrecking ball dangling from a crane and brutalizing the wall of the building adjacent to the one in which I'd been lodged. Good. At least I wasn't going nuts.

My Twingo—manufactured by Renault—was one of those tiny, clutch-less, stick-shift Euro-Rental cars. I had parked it half on the street and half on the sidewalk. I got in, pretended that the parking job had been intentional when a passersby tsk-tsked me, and drove off, headed somewhere, anywhere away from the evil ball and piss-fumed room.

Two hours and four espressos later I arrived in the middle of nowhere. I had been going east, maybe south a little, and had ended up on a red-dirt tree-lined country lane and surrounded by fields of lavender and copses of willows. Here in nowhere were a cat-tailed pond, a farmhouse, and a dilapidated French hay-barn.

The Twingo died. Why? I had no idea. I coasted to the side of the road and tried to avoid a ditch. When I got out of the car, I nearly cried, swept away by the fresh air, zephyred grasses, and most of all, the silence. I leaned against the carcass of the Twingo and closed my eyes and let the sunlight wash over my face. I sensed the places the sunlight touched on my body and the places it didn't, and how the warmth soothed my aching calf. I vigorously rubbed my hair and scalp to dislodge imagined lice. My old-school flip phone had died and lay on the dash under the glass windshield as useless as Lenin's body in Red Square.

At the end of a plane tree bordered driveway was a white manor with a slated mansard roof and green shuttered windows, some of which opened and faced an adjacent pond. I left my bag in the Twingo and walked up the drive. An older woman greeted me.

"Bonjour, Monsieur. La voiture en panne? C'est une voiture de location?"

Cottonmouth. I bit at flakes of skin on my lips. "Yes, a rental. It's . . .broken. My phone is dead. Could I trouble you to call the rental company, or a mechanic?"

"Pas aujourd'hui," she explained. "C'est le week-end. Peut-être lundi."

She went on to explain that there was only one mechanic nearby and he did contract work for all the major rental companies. I understood, of course. The weekend meant no mechanic. The French take their weekends seriously. Too exhausted to speak, especially to speak French, I sighed a long, dry sigh.

"Suis-moi," the woman ordered.

I followed as instructed. She was in her 70s or 80s, so she had license to use the familiar *tu* form. She took my arm, unfazed by my disheveled state, and helped me to a chair in a spotlessly clean, country kitchen with a white and black tiled floor. The cool surface of the tile penetrated the soles of my shoes. En route to the house, we had made introductions. Madame Cottin, Liliane Cottin was her name. She asked that I call her Liliane, not the more respectful Madame Cottin.

She disappeared behind me—I didn't follow her motions—and returned with a damp towel so I could wipe off my hands and face. The second round, she returned with two pitchers, one with hot coffee and another with warm milk—café au lait. My next wish came true: bread, marmalade, and butter appeared. She said little to nothing. I think she understood that I couldn't carry my side of a conversation. The realization didn't bother her. Nor was she bothered by me, a stranger, a foreigner in desperate need of a shower, being in her house. I saw no one else on the premises and assumed, and later confirmed, that she lived alone.

I jumped when she removed the towel from the table and put her hand on my shoulder. She knelt beside me, rolled up my bloodied pant leg, and used the damp towel to clean around the cut on my calf.

"Mieux," she looked at her work and announced satisfaction.

Her touch had been purposeful—a nurse or doctor? She left me to finish my café and bread, for which I thanked her, and then returned with a gauze and tape, blanket, linens, and towels. Again, I was directed to follow. I obliged and was led to a spacious upstairs bedroom. I glimpsed a claw-foot tub in the adjacent bathroom. See-through ceiling-to-floor curtains covered French doors and access to a half-balcony with a wrought-iron railing. She nodded to a clock hanging on the wall. My gaze went to the clock, then followed her as she pushed aside the curtains and opened the doors to a view of tilled fields and woodlands.

"On dîne à vingt heures." The tone implied one shouldn't be late. Having nothing more, she left, quietly closing the door behind her.

I learned who the "on" was when we dined. Liliane. No husband, no other family, no cooks or cleaners. She had prepared lapin à la moutarde—rabbit cooked with Dijon mustard—and then poured a local Viognier from Condrieu region, a nine-mile stretch, she explained, of wineries and vineyards along the banks of the Rhône. The unlabeled bottle, she added, was from a neighbor who didn't like being told what to do with his vines.

On Monday, as promised, she arranged for a mechanic. After a ten-minute inspection of the Twingo, he informed us that he had to order a part, I forget what part, and would return Thursday or Friday. I asked the mechanic if I might ride back to town with him and stay at a hotel in town. Liliane had been translating and I missed a good part of what she said. The mechanic's reply to my question was definitive: "Non."

The next surprise followed directly.

"Tu sais cuisiner?" she asked.

"Yes, I know how to cook," I answered. "Actually, I enjoy cooking."

"Bon."

With that, I received a tour of the kitchen, a guided inspection of the contents of the fridge, a brief visit to a cellar stocked with wine, bottled vegetables and fruits, and boxes of root vegetables. The milk truck would drop off milk, cream, eggs, and cheese. Following the tour, Liliane informed me that friends were picking her up for a week of things il faut faire à Paris—and that I was welcome to stay until the Twingo was fixed and ready to go. Should there be an emergency, my phone was charged and her auto, an old Mercedes, was in the barn. In tidy, cursive script she wrote out various contact numbers.

This time she spoke in a mix of French and English. The accent was thick.

"You must stay. I want you to stay, rester. Ici—*here* in French—ici is le Centre du Silence. The same in English," she said. "The Center of Silence."

She handed me a yellowed-with-age copy of Rousseau's *Les Rèveries du Promeneur Solitaire* and was gone within the hour.

What followed were days of quiet and calm. I lost count because she was gone longer than expected and the Twingo repaired later than expected. I imagined myself like Rousseau, driven to the countryside by detractors and a deep desire for pause and reflection, dreaming and revelry. I swapped worldly concerns for a quotidian routine of café au lait and croissants, une promenade matinale à la Jean-Jacques Rousseau, and an early dinner with Madame's Larousse dictionary, during which I slogged through *Les Rêveries* and became reacquainted with French's literary past tenses and moods. About nine p.m., as the sun withdrew, I would bathe, and then sleep as long as I cared, often more than ten hours.

After the Twingo had been fixed and my bags mostly packed, I stayed on. I worked on my translations and noticed, and didn't care, that the Nokia had lost its charge. I didn't want to leave the house unattended or in a disarray, so tidying up became part of the routine, as did stockpiling wood for the fireplace. I even did a little weeding in the garden.

Liliane returned. She surveyed the place and pronounced it in satisfactory condition. She asked if I felt better —I did, thank you—and we made our goodbyes. I thanked her again, promising to keep in touch but both of us knowing that would not be the case. I gathered my bag and passed a side-table I had to have walked by dozens of times. This time I noticed a framed photo, black and white and stained with age, a portrait of a cocky-looking young man in a jaunty beret, recognizable even now as Albert Renard-Maes. That gentleman, my recent acquaintance from Chateaux d'Œx, had written in a neat hand and in ink, now faded, the following words: *à Lily, mon amour, ma vie, mon tout.*

Sauvage: / so.vaʒ / adjective / wild, untamed

Manzanita

The family's Thanksgiving call's dénouement had been uneventful.

A month passed without a word from Elaine, Kali, or Zadie. Not even a Christmas card. Intentional or not, the ghosting was well-deserved payback. I'd de facto ghosted my own family for years.

Hence the shock and awe when this text popped up on my phone: <<ZP: Papa Otto. What's your address? I'm at the airport?>>

<<OP: What airport!!!>>

<<ZP: Portland>>

I didn't want to believe it: <<OP: Your Portland or mine?>>

<<ZP: Yours, silly!>>

<<OP: Why?>>

<<ZP: I was reading The Little Prince, and I thought to myself, I'm going to visit Papa Otto. You know, when it counts. Before I become a grown-up. Took the red eye.>>

I wanted to unleash a string of emojis but I lacked the skills. A texter's eternity passed.

<<ZP: You there?>>

Too late. I can't leave granddaughter stuck in a city I had recently declared uninhabitable.

<<OP: I'm not in Portland. Sorry.>>

That did result in a flurry of emojis, none of which I understood, especially their compounded meaning. It's teen Chinese.

<<OP: I moved to Manzanita. two-hour drive. I'll come get you.>>

It was my turn to wait. I considered immediately calling Kali but feared losing the connection with Zadie.

<<ZP: Got it. Manzanita by Cannon Beach. Catching the Red Line. Be there in 4 hrs.>>

<<OP: Wait—>>

<<ZP: Don't call Mom!! I'll call her when I get there. No time to explain.>>

That was it. Silence. I should call Kali. But Zadie was already in Oregon; the reckoning could wait, and there was laundry to do and to put away. No one wants to see gramp's skivvies hanging on a drying rack in the living room.

Manzanita is a beach community of 700 or so permanent residents. The "or so" means the number is fluid, influenced by the Portland diaspora caused by Covid, homelessness, and trash, and more trash. I'm an escapee who is yet to be vetted by the locals. I'm local enough to know that the crank is good at Manzanita News and Espresso. That's where the bus will drop off Zadie. The News is across the street from the police department. A convenient location in multiple respects.

The town is a somewhat liberal island in a red swamp. The Covid effect has played out here like elsewhere. Relatively well-off city dwellers have driven up real estate prices, along with remote working dot-com millennials, real estate hustlers, and business owners. The average Joe and Jill have been displaced, and with them, much of the young work force. A cynic would argue that the community farms, parades, fairs, and farmers' markets are picturesque remakes of more genuinely rural times. That's not the case, though, and these happenings continue to foster a sense of community and joy. The idiots running around with red hats and without masks and gearing up for the apocalypse add to the local color. Buy a gun, they say. I agree, for once, and have several.

I think Manzanita has a disproportionate number of gays and I have a number friends here who are gay. If Zadie stays for more than a cameo, she will find a supportive community that understands sexual identity issues better than I do.

No one speaks French in Manzanita except people of a certain age who have in the past paid une raçon de roi to the Alliance Française for lessons. I tutor French. It pays bills and keeps me in Bob's Red Mill flour for homemade sourdough. I drive a beater Subaru and rent a seven-hundred-square-foot cottage a block from the beach.

Rain or shine, every day, and sometimes at night, I walk or jog a couple miles along the beach. I watch and smell the sea, follow the ebb and flow of the tides and sea life, and track the phases of the moon. I think often of my parents. They loved me. I don't doubt it now, but I had questioned their love for most of my life. I am one year older than my father was when he died. Funny, no . . . tragic, that it took so long to understand that my many shortcomings were not my parents' doing.

Disconnect

My mother's eyes were brown and generous. She died when I was nineteen, after I had moved to Colorado. I returned to Cicero to witness her two-week arc toward death, a passage that was forever for a teen but a sigh for a seventy-something. She was forty-eight. Her passing was marked by the little hand and the big hand counting down the hours on the ubiquitous black and white hospital wall clock; her life was marked by the morning shifts at the family café. She opened the joint at six a.m. and went by the name "Whitey" because she had platinum blonde hair. She was so much more than a waitressing machine without a real name. So much more. She had a distance about her, like me.

After my mother's death and for the duration of the next year my father and I abided each other's company. Mostly, we hid in our personal guilt-riddled gulags: He for having worked Mom to death in the business and for never having been honest with me about not being my biological father; and me, for abandoning my parents when I should have stepped up and appreciated all that they had done for me.

Mom had switched insurance companies right before she got sick. The paperwork took two weeks to process. Within those two weeks, her cancer had been discovered and she had died. Unbelievable. That's why I stuck around. Out of pride or shame, people in those days paid their bills. Dad worked, though too old to work. I loaded semi-trailers at a local trucking outfit, slug cases of OJ for another delivery company in the early a.m., and TA'd math at a community college where I took a couple classes. My father worked nights. We did nothing but work. The pay-down took a year. We hardly spoke to each other, rarely ate a meal together, and never once socialized together. In the end, bills paid, we went our separate ways, deceptions untarnished.

When my father passed, he had insurance. Took two weeks for him, too. In those days people were efficient at dying. Dad didn't have a will, but on his deathbed and using his last few breaths he whispered what he wanted done with the few assets he had. He had sold our home and was living off the cash. He trusted me to disburse the remaining funds. I fulfilled my obligations exactly as requested.

In his later years, he had been befriended by two women, a Jew and a Babushka. The Bohemian had been my mother's best friend; the Jewish woman my father's. Right after his passing, the women ransacked his apartment for anything of value. That's what Dad had wanted, for them to take whatever they wanted. I watched, emotionless, like I was watching the tele. Greedy chicken eyes ogled contents of one drawer after another, occasionally sharing a tear or squinty smile. I watched. I'm not much attached to material shit. It was the emotional experience that stuck with me.

The pièce de résistance of my father's funeral was a visit to the funeral parlor by my soon-to-be mother-in-law and her drinking buddy. Two women again, this time wealthy Midwestern wasps tipsy from afternoon martinis and amused by the kitschy Bohunk funeral, the open casket, the fake flowers, and working-class attendees. An old man placed one hand on my father's chest and rested the other on the billowy, satin coffin liner. His coarse skin snagged the fabric. Grime rimmed his fingernails. "Rest in peace, Harold," he said. They were words from a loyal, long-time customer and friend who was paying his respects.

This guy I knew. He ran Cicero's garbage company and was probably worth millions. The mob backed the business. He had given my dad a make-work watchman job. Harold needed 'somethin' ta do,' y' know, the man said. I could imagine him and Dad shootin' the breeze. He sized me up but didn't say what he thought: where the fuck have you been, punk?

The WASPs buzzed the fake flowers.

Yeah, I thought on that 'somethin' ta do.' My dad and I could have done a lot more than we did—he could have been a father and I could have been a son. A painful thing to see yourself through other's eyes.

Elaine and I married soon after my father's death. Ours was a marriage founded on love, pride, and guilt. I felt guilty about knocking her up and she felt guilty about everything. We raised a child, our Kali. But it wasn't a cakewalk and the whole fucking world seemed to know about our *difficulties* before I did. I still resent that.

We were in love and too young and stupid to admit that maybe we'd made a big fucking mistake. Or maybe that's how it is for everyone. We yoked up for a twenty-year slog down a road paved in wishful thinking. Her moneyed family smoothed over bumps and ruts and provided distractions.

Who was I kidding? My friends asked, "What took you so long?"—referring to our divorce and the humiliation we had each endured for years. Elaine's friends asked the same question of her, repeatedly reminding her that hubby was a womanizing, self-centered asshole. Our friends got it right and they got it wrong. What was it that kept us together? Was it the idea of love, the kids, a faux reality, or something what Elaine and I stole from each other? Much of the time we hung on opposite ends of rope draped over a razor's edge. We were afraid to move and we were not happy.

I'm certain that the hundred plus guests who attended our high society wedding knew that we were a doomed couple. The wedding was like a shareholders' meeting where Elaine and Otto were certified 'happy ever after' by a super-majority of the guest list. The show went on though neither of us could say why. We weren't ready for marriage and by the time we were ready, the connection had worn thin. We got good at saying I love you on the phone, hanging up, and going about our individual lives. We had an "arrangement." Mine involved other women. Hers involved something else, an intentional distancing, a something I've never understood and never will.

There's a pattern of hurt, isn't there, a disconnect with my parents and with my wife, even my daughter. Gee, I wonder why? And with Zadie?

Chamonix

Some years into our marriage I took a guiding gig in Chamonix, France, the heart of alpine climbing in Europe. In those days, in the U.S., all one needed to be certified as a guide was to have a paying client. Europe, on the other hand, had strict standards. Even so, if a U.S. guide were a decent climber with a decent rep, he or she got the royal guide treatment in Europe. This meant a degree of popularity, a discount on the téléphérique, cheap food at the at-that-time-rat-hole Bar Nash (Brasserie le National), and cheap rates at the Auberge de L'Avre, a hotel that had always looked better on paper than in the flesh but, to its credit, the L'Avre did offer a stunning view of Mont Blanc and the Aiguille du Midi. A big plus: the restaurant served delicious, warm pots of milk and coffee at breakfast—the best café au lait ever.

In the spring and fall, I'd take a couple clients for a month-long guided climbing experience. I continued this practice even after I became a venture capital associate and juggled conference calls with the time change and my guiding schedule. My work away from work was a break from career pressure and from duties as a husband and father. The clients and I would hole up in Cham, fail to climb Mt. Blanc because the weather always sucked, and then I'd convince my brood that we should go to the Dolomites where we'd get up a few routes for real. The change of venue always came with a hiatus in the climbing and gave my clients a chance to spend a few days in

Venice—without me. I was paid regardless. Post-Venice we would rendezvous in Cortina d'Ampezzo.

Those socked-in weeks in Chamonix were special—as in Mariel special. Twenty-something, blonde hair grazing the shoulders and thin fingers good for working the till at the front desk of Auberge de L'Arve. Though reserved and professional, Mariel wore scandalously tight jeans (for those days). She was related to the owners. They tolerated the tight pants because she was family and because she never missed a charge on the guests' factures. The first time I saw her she was wearing a suede green jacket with big black plastic buttons. The coat hung flat across the front of her torso. There was a belt on the back with a black button on each end. The way the belt was attached tucked in the waist.

I was trying, with poor result, to get through a dual language edition of Madame Bovary. Mariel's attire called up the scene where Bovary's son is ridiculed for his clothes by his classmates on his first day of class. Any resemblance of Mariel to either Charles or Mme Bovary ended after chapter one.

Mariel was engaged to a soldier. Soldier Boy—she never told me his name, calling him only mon soldat—was always somewhere that was not Chamonix. Was the missing fiancé a fiction to fend off the riffraff? Un type imaginaire. On my first trip to Cham, the third day, clients in their rooms and me bored and the only customer at the four-stool bar, Mariel left her post at the front desk and sat next to me. She ordered us eau de vie poire. She used English every day but her vocabulary was limited to hotel-speak. I think she was hoping to pick up some English from le guide américain who, par chance, also had shoulder-length hair.

We tried English. However, as is always the case when people genuinely want to communicate with each other, we shifted to our strongest common language, in this case, French. I was enthralled by her unhurried, soft, Marseille Provençal dialect, sans swallowed syllables or stranded vowels, and avec shadows of Baudelaire and Rimbaud. She gave every sentence and every word its full due. I'm naturally breezy, a cover for my insecurities and, as I learned, a counterproductive habit when conversing with Mariel. Parle lentement, parle clairement—speak slowly, speak clearly. Her mantra.

Several brandies later we had one of those intellectual epiphanies people who drink too much have and decided that fidelity to spouses and fiancés only mattered when one was indoors. In wild nature, in one's soul, there arose irrepressible and primitive impulses that had been imprinted in our DNA over tens of thousands of years. One had no choice.

"Je veux dire, nous sommes . . . animaux!" she declared.

We further decided that *anyplace* outside or outdoors counted as wild nature, and congratulated ourselves on a second shared revelation. You would think that this was flirtatious, tipsy, bar talk. It wasn't. And Mariel was no Mme Bovary. Not a mote of self-doubt or hesitancy in that girl. She warned me from the get-go, first in English: "I. Do. Not. Go. Halfway." Then in French: "Je vais jusqu'au bout."The words gave me goosebumps.

Two blocks from Auberge de L'Avre the still narrow Rive Arve wove through the middle of Chamonix. The tinted silt-green waters drained Mont Blanc's Mer de Glace and met up with the Rhone eighty kilometers to the north-west in Geneva. Forty-plus years ago, when I was in Cham, the parks outnumbered outlet stores and a treed boardwalk and a waist-high wrought iron balustrade lined the river.

Mariel pressed the palms of her hands on the metal railing and leaned forward to look at the river. The reflection of the hunched moon bobbled on the water's surface. Overhead lay a frozen strata of stars and cloud. Our exhalations took on animal shapes. I pressed against her from behind, but then quickly stopped, fearful of the prospect of the rail giving way and tumbling into the icy water. Mariel, in agreement, turned and led me to a harsh-barked oak. She put her back to its trunk, pulled me close: "Rien à mis-chemin." We kissed un-tenderly, like I imagine folks on Tinder might dream about, teeth gnashing and lips getting bruised.

Never on that night, nor the many that followed, did our intentions require interpretation. Wild nature ruled. We set up a tent at a local campground and named it Chez Sauvage. Was it ridiculous to fuck in a tent when we each had a nice room with a real bed at the Auberge? Sure. What aroused her most were days when I'd roll in after twelve hours of guiding, smelling like fear and sweat, with a dirty butt and day-old breath.

Mariel, to her credit, was as careful about keeping our trysts as secret as she was eager to have them. I recall not one phone call, one message, or a single letter between us. For three years and five trips to Cham, the routine never varied. Le Soldat was always wherever Le Soldat was—perhaps the Légion Étrangère. I would arrive and Mariel would set up the tent and stock it with blankets, a puff, condoms, water, wine and random leftovers from the L'Avre restaurant. Thus segregated from the civilized world, we conducted our savage love-making. She preferred all fours, even like dogs really do—which, I tell you, is a trick. The girl had a kinky edge and I went with it. Mariel claimed: je ne peux pas jouir face à face, insisting once, after a face à face, that the salty bog between her legs was all me. Yes, ma brute, if you say so.

The dynamic changed in the fall trip on year three. Often I'd fail her. I blamed my anxiety on the experience with Jock and fear that one night Le Soldat would peel back the tent flap and shove the barrel of a gun between my teeth. It had taken forever to say this in French and I probably got across a fraction of what

I'd intended to say. The admission embarrassed me, not because of my wanting French but because the explanation was only half-true. The other half was that wife and I had never clicked physically—no blame here, just a statement of fact—and that each year our connection had been emptier than the last. Many couples successfully accommodated such differences. We, however, did not. Indeed, some years later, after we had given up trying to fix things, Elaine delivered a welcomed coup de grâce to our wounded marriage and divorced me. When on that night, still years before the divorce, I told Mariel, she instantly grasped the fatal trajectory of my marriage.

She started in English. "You are alien."

"Huh?" I intelligently replied, proving I wasn't an alien.

"Tu es détaché de l'amour."

"Alienated?"

"Oui, alliéné. Avec tout le monde."

She cocked her head to side. Her eyes glistened. Then she hugged me so hard that her nipples left bruises my chest. After the bone crushing hug, she shoved me off and laughed. Her mouth grew wide and leonine and I had this vision like she was going to take me in her jaws and carry me off into the night. A strange, scary, Oedipal image that. I wondered if she thought I had made up the story about Jock. What the hell had I actually said in French? Another "tant pis" miscue? I'll never know.

That fall the weather in Cham was perfect. One splitter day followed another; there was no Venice interruptus for my clients. Mariel and I set up camp as usual and hung out together as much as my guiding and her concierging allowed. We joked about sex and had a couple of playful forays, but no savage lovemaking. Our tent and campsite continued to serve as a sanctuary from the world and its worries. Our last night together, like our first, was frosty and starry. We huddled under a blanket, smiled, and laughed at nothing. We drank hot cocoas laced with pear brandy. I looked a Mariel, tried to imagine what she was thinking and gave up. I thought about Carole and "the best is later." I'd never felt closer to Mariel than that night.

I never said a word about our affair. I don't think Mariel did either. After year three, I stopped guiding in Europe. We've not spoken since. I once inquired about Mariel with a guide-friend who works in Chamonix. He said Mariel was still there, her once blonde hair is shoulder length and now more grey than blond. She seemed happy, he reported, and now owns and manages Auberge L'Avre and another boutique hotel in town. Money and love destroyed Mme. Bovary; Mariel, au contraire, did well for herself.

My guide friend made no mention of Le Soldat. I suspect Mariel has been as circumspect about her marriage as she had been about our affair. I did not ask my friend to inquire or say hello.

Heureux: / œ.ʁø / adj. masc. sing. / happy

The Sea

My Manzanita rental, built in 1937, was a wood-shingled beach house with weathered blue shutters in need of paint. Heat came from a black-bellied stove that mainlined wood pellets. One couldn't see the surf, so the rent was reasonable. But I heard the water's roar. At king tides, the sound intimidated.

High tide was approaching, though not a king tide. Fickle winds whipped the shore. No kite-boarders today. And no surfers. No one surfed here because there wasn't a single, decent break in the seven miles of beach between Neahkahnie Mountain and the Nehalem Bay jetty.

Zadie flicked off her mask as she bounced down the steps of the colorful, hippie-era school bus that had been repurposed as the official Manzanita-Portland commuter. The driver handed down her luggage. My concern that an awkward moment would arise if she didn't recognize me turned out to be unfounded. She found me before her foot touched the ground. I waited. A wise grandparent always lets the grandchild set the pace. A mile-wide grin had been waiting under that mask. She walked up and gave me a huge hug, a human moment in this Covid era, and an act that erased any worry I had about the status of our relationship.

After, I extended my arms but still held her by the shoulders. I noted how much she had grown and the inroads of maturity at the corners of her eyes. Her top front tooth was noticeably chipped. As an easily embarrassed boy, I'd played hooky from school the day after I chipped a front tooth.

I cocked my head to the side to get a better look at the tooth. Most kids today had perfect teeth.

"Hockey," she said. Without my asking, she added, "I kinda like the look."

"So," I asked. I wanted to get off on the right foot. "Is it Zadie or Zack?"

"Whatever, Papa Otto. I mean I care, but with you I really don't care. What's more comfortable for you?"

"Zadie is what I'm used to. And you—whatever the name— are the person I love and support one-gazillion percent."

Zadie's eyes glistened.

"Look, Papa Otto. I don't know what the fuck I'm—"

"You know," I interrupted, "Hippocrates said sexual identity was a point on a continuum between male and female. And anyone could be anywhere on that continuum. Science agrees. And your Papa Otto agrees."

Having just read this claim in the Times, I was comfortable putting it out there.

I continued. "Moreover, you do not have to label yourself. Not for me, not for anybody, not today, and not ten years from now."

"That's not exactly what I was looking for, but I'll take it." She gave me two thumbs up. I wiped off a tear rolling down her cheek.

One rolled down mine. Zadie dabbed at it with the cuff of her jacket. The material was abrasive. Were it not so cold and my face already reddened, Zadie would have noticed my embarrassment at my presumption that her question had been about gender identity and not simply why she was here. Note to self: A grandparent should not be presumptive.

Zadie let the matter pass. "Papa Otto, you're all scruffles—"

"Yup. Haven't shaved in a couple. When in Rome . . ."

Zadie checked out Rome. I followed her gaze. Every man in view had a beard. Welcome to Oregon. I introduced Zadie to a bushy, gay couple having coffees and standing under an umbrella at the News. The rain had recommenced. The beards on both men hid their necks and crawled upward into nostrils and ears. A gust flagged the beards and, in unison, the men grabbed them.

I'll stick with a stubble. Enough facial hair to camouflage the erosion of age and, when I laughed, soften hardened features.

"We can walk to my place from here."

We turned off Laneda, the main drag and one of the few streets in Manzanita with a sidewalk and walked single file up First Street. Zadie had packed a waist-high roller-bag. I took it from her. Our three forms made the same angle to the wind. A wheel squeaked. We didn't speak.

"I want to swim in the ocean." Zadie declared.

"Nobody swims in the ocean here. Even in summer. It's bloody cold and the chop's dangerous."

The Arctic current prowls the shoreline. Chop, rip tides, and unpredictable—as the name implies—sneaker waves compound the unpleasantries. Oregon kite-boarders armor themselves in neoprene, helmets, and life-vests. The undertows are impossible to predict and always present.

"Dip toes-in-sand. Be happy with toes-in-sand—" I suggested.

"Where's my room?"

"I hadn't exactly prepared a room for you," I said. Though, for an hour, I had done just that.

I pointed to the only extra room in the house. It had a bench-bed and a separate door to the shared bathroom. The house was dated but the furniture was Ikea circa 2015. Zadie disappeared for ten minutes and then emerged with pink crocs on her feet and wrapped in a white bath towel. The black one-piece women's Speedo reminded me that Zadie was a competitive swimmer. Goggles and a black bathing cap imprinted with a U.S. flag dangled from her fingers. We headed for the beach. Let it be a learning experience, I told myself.

"It's getting dark." I warned.

"Plenty of time. I see the beach! C'mon!"

A narrow, sandy footpath parted waist-high dune grass that had been combed to one side by the offshore breeze. Sand particles pricked our flesh. Zadie strode passed the debris-laden wrack line and onto the open beach. She dropped the towel and kicked off the crocs. A moment later the towel lifted off the ground. I snagged it mid-flight and packed it under my arm.

Raw as it was, Zadie owned the cold. The grains of sand and droplets of rain that smote her pale flesh simply hardened her resolve. She watched and breathed in the rhythm of the surf, like she was taking its measure.

To the north, clouds sieged the upper reaches of Neahkahnie Mountain. To the south, a mist shrouded the jetty at the inlet to Nehalem Bay. The beach was uninhabited save us and, a hundred meters toward the jetty, a young couple holding hands. Like me, they had bundled up in windbreaker and hoodie.

A veil of sand and fist-sized globs of sea foam flowed underfoot. Wave-chasing sanderlings plowed sand at the break's edge for grubs. Their spindly legs swish-swished at eighty-words-a-minute across the tide-washed sand and left tracks like runes that vanished with each wave.

"Is that pollution stuff?" Zadie yelled over the wind.

I'd been reading up and talking to locals. I knew the answer and shook my head, no. "They're skeletons of dead phytoplankton, like bubbles of phytoplankton." My benumbed lips had said something closer to bite-o-bank-in. "The wind strips them from the surface of the water."

My nose runs when it's windy and cold. And I drool. I used the back of my hand to wipe away the saliva and snot.

"Sorry," I said. The polite was unnecessary.

Arms akimbo, Zadie marched seaward. Everybody watched. Everybody being me, the couple, and a cluster of sanderlings ready to bolt.

I had expected her to charge the water, briefly frolic in knee-high surf, and then scurry back with the sneaping froth at her heals.

My sneakers squished in ankle-deep water. Zadie never flinched, never stood on her toes, and never squealed.

Water in the low fifties was deadly, although one could get used to it. Would I be able to rescue her if a wave took her? I had rescued Mlle Lachenal, but then I had been both young and a confident swimmer. But who was I kidding? Changing "had been" into "am" fifty-years on was folly. I'd end up a statistic, another example of why they warn you to never try to save someone caught in the Oregon surf. Fear of shaming, however, is stronger than fear of death. I would plunge, even if it killed me, even as I visualized a seized heart, lungs craving oxygen, and the icy burn of saltwater in the throat.

I'd recently dreamt that I would die on December fourteenth, five years hence. That oddly comforting certitude lingered like a memory of the future, and I thought, well, maybe I would survive a rescue attempt.

Zadie stepped into the first wave, then stepped back to recalibrate for the next. She crouched, tensed, and dove into a four-foot-tall frothing cascade of water.

Years ago I'd taken a swim in San Francisco Bay with a couple members of the Dolphin Club. The water had been sixty-one degrees, a temperature for which insulated swim caps and earplugs were considered mandatory. If the inner ear goes numb, one can become disoriented. I should have told Zadie to stuff something in her ears and given her a liner for her swim cap.

I waited and watched. Nothing. A long minute later, thirty yards out, I saw an arm. I waded ten feet forward, not taking my eyes off the spot where I'd seen her. A wave slammed into my thighs. I didn't feel the cold and swallowed the bile in my throat.

Another eternal minute passed. The drama ended when, like a revenant, Zadie strode through a wall of water. We saw each other, my face frozen with concern and hers wearing a wide, chip-toothy grin that made my heart pound.

The sun broke through the clouds. Light bounced off moon jellies strewn across the dark wet sand.

Zadie emerged from the turbulence as composed as Botticelli's Venus. The top half of her one-piece was tucked in at the waist. Why? Was that intentional or had it been a wave? Her flesh was red, like it had been slapped by the sea. Her goggles hung loosely around her neck. She wore a nasty scrape on the shoulder like a bloody epaulet. This being, indomitable and androgynous walked toward me with muscled grace. This was Zadie 2.0, Zadie unfiltered, Zadie in command.

Like good Hora I draped a towel across Zadie's shoulders. She made the towel into a carapace and held it in place with clenched fists.

The drama now over, the couple turned away, fumbled for each other's hands, and recommenced their walk. What would they say tonight about the person they had seen enter and emerge from the surf? Nuts to go in the water like that! Was it a he or she?

"That was so freakin' wild." The blue lips mouthed the words with difficulty. Zadie freed one arm, snorted saltwater out of each nostril—making me think, again, about Mlle Lachenal. She reached to sky and hopped around in circle. "Yes! Wow! Yes!"

I watched and smiled, amazed and a little envious. I'd forgotten what it was like to feel like that.

We made our way up the dune in clumsy uneven steps, walking arm in arm. The surf's pounding shook windows along Ocean Road. The wind toyed with the tops of trees.

I turned my head to face Zadie, so she could hear me. "Casi."

"Casi?"

My arm was around her shoulder; I was careful to not touch where the abrasion was. A half-block inland we no longer needed to yell.

"Casi is short for Casimir. From Casimir Pulaski. Revolutionary War hero—here and in Poland. I read he saved George Washington's life and that he was a dashing, cavalry officer."

"Casimir was—" I paused to think about how to rephrase what I had been about to say, and then thought it better to say nothing.

"I'm doing it again, Zadie. Having conversation in my head and jumping into stuff I'm projecting. I'm sorry."

"Just say it. Let me decide."

"Okay. Well, I also read that Casimir was biologically intersex."

That had been a hard thing for me to say and right after I said it I chided myself.

First, I was ignorant and insensitive about this stuff. The notion of sexual identity had evolved to become a complex of gender identities. My trans and gay friends drew distinctions about how one thought of oneself, how a person wanted to appear to others, who one desired and how one wanted to be desired. I had zip personal experience with such nuances and really ought to shut up.

And second, Zadie had not come to Manzanita to be bombed with my ideas about how she might live her life. She'd gotten plenty of that bullshit at home. I was being as inconsiderate as Kali and Earl, maybe even reactive.

"Uh-huh. Sex stuff aside, I like Casi," she said.

We walked slowly and looked for traffic although there was none.

"Me, too." I tried to recover. "Hey, I'm sorry. Not my business, okay"

"Seems a thing. My happiness being other people's business. I'll think about it."

Parsley

The hissing from the stove merged the drone of the surf. After our outdoor adventure and tension I felt from our conversation, I needed a jigger of Cragganmore.

There was a voice message from daughter Kali. Per Kali, Zadie had made a cameo in Aspen, Earl had come down hard on her about 'acting' like a boy, and Zadie had left the next day without a goodbye or a note. Kali called the few friends Zadie had in Aspen and got a scripted response: "Oh, she was just here. So sorry, I don't know where she is right now. If I see her I'll tell her you called." Wisely, Kali checked credit cards for travel charges but came up empty.

Kali leaves epic phone messages. As a rule, I don't listen and simply call back when I have a chance. This message I listened to. The saga continued. Zadie had been put on probation and could be expelled for an incident—a fight—at Penobscot Academy. Kali's concerns were justified.

Zadie had been clever, using cash and asking friends to cover for her. Was I happy that she had been standing up for herself? Sure. Was I worried about her? A shitload more, yes.

I thought about the row with Earl and the fight at school, and I realized that I knew next to nothing about decisions Zadie had made or was making regarding gender identity. I'd never even thought to question my gender identity or its origin. What normative references did she have for what she felt inside? What trusted arguments or evidence could she use to say and believe that I'm an x, y, or z. What did "trans" mean to her? Certainly, it was more than putting on a pair trousers.

I stared at my phone and looked back at the train wreck of choices I had made when I had been her age. Zadie was so much more mature, but not an adult. I deleted Kali's message and jumped when Zadie walked into the room. "Can I taste?"

She had changed into Levi's, flannel shirt, and "Patagucci" vest. Earlier, I'd tossed her Covid-tainted travel wear into the clothes washer.

"How 'bout a wee splash of your own?"

The invite surprised. "Wow! Sure. Thanks, Papa Otto."

That's what grandparents do: Corrupt the grandchildren. Pass the hemlock, I'm short! I'm addled. With faux impunity I poured a half-jigger and handed it to her. She took the glass. My fingers were ice; hers like toast.

We didn't wait for a round of easy chit-chat before addressing the elephant in the beach house.

"So why, Zadie whom I dearly love and admire, are you here? Certainly not to listen to me pontificate!"

"Kinda obvious, Papa Otto. To see you! Just hang."

To be **yourself** is what flitted through my brain. Let Zadie talk. The single malt was helping.

"Mom know?"

"Kinda sorta . . ."

"So. No."

"She knows I'm not in school. But it's my study abroad quarter!"

I was surprised, given Covid, that any school, especially Zadie's conservative prep school, would risk students traveling abroad. Also odd was that the foreign study program had not been mentioned in the family call. And lastly, I had been led to believe that everything was hunky-dory at Penobscot. Be a self-involved asshole and that's all you get. Step up, Otto.

Zadie swished the whisky around. She was taking time to get her story straight.

"And where would that be, your study abroad?" I asked.

"Lausanne, Switzerland. The program is so cool, a total immersion thing. I stay with this family—they're really nice, I've talked to them—and nobody speaks English . . . I mean, they do, but they won't when I'm there."

"I see. When do you leave?"

"Well, that's the thing. I'm not going. I can't. Not for a while. Can't even fly there. Pandemic and all. Mom and Earl weren't keen on it anyway. You don't care what they—"

"I do care . . ." Damnit, I did want to know.

Zadie had a noisy sip before speaking. "Mom was worried about the travel part. And Earl said it was a waste of time."

"Really? A waste of time?"

"Yeah, being in Europe, learning French."

Zadie pushed her head forward. She lowered her jaw and her voice, imitating Earl. "Whaddya gonna learn from them Franchies that you can't learn here!" She resumed in her normal voice, "I mean, I don't think he knows Lausanne is in Switzerland!"

For the hundredth time, I asked myself why my otherwise intelligent daughter was with this jerk. Though, in Earl's defense, he knows damned well where Lausanne is. On the other hand, he's an idiot about medical matters. I knew Zadie had been vaccinated, even boosted. Earl, of course, didn't want to be told what to do. I should break his leg. Sorry, man. I just felt like breaking your fucking leg.

"And—"

She cut me off. "I'm doing the next best thing."

"Québec?" I joked. A stupid comment.

Zadie's was excited to tell me. I could see it in her eyes. She downed the remainder of her drink like a sailor and asked for another. I gave in but made it half the volume of the previous drink. I gave myself a bartender's jigger.

"I think maybe my program will be . . ." She looked sideward and scrunched her eyes, pretending, like she was thinking hard about what she was about to say, "a partial-immersion thing. The plan is that I always speak French at home. And study and read only French books and watch French tele. See, my phone is all set up for French!" Zadie showed me her iPhone and then dug around in her daypack and pulled out Le Petit Prince. *I could just make out the title in the dim light from the pellet stove. The days felt short. Shorter than when I was young. Shorter than when I didn't have cataracts.*

It was obvious where this conversation was going. I asked anyway. "And where would this special program take place?"

She looked at me like I couldn't add two and two. Never a bad guess, that.

I waited. Her eyes lit up, her whole face lit up when she delivered the coup de grace en français: "Ici!"

I'd expected that answer but not my skipped heartbeat.

"I see!" I said, although in my ears the 'I see' echoed the ici. " Are you sure you can—and really want—to stay here for . . ."

"—six semaines."

Six weeks wasn't that long. However, I would be a crusty companion. Old men are set in their ways, especially old men who live alone. I have my rituals and I like them. Did I really just admit that to myself! I didn't even want a dog, especially not one of those fluffy little white things that every third retiree here has. Fucking shark bait.

"I'd love if you stayed with me. I doubt Kali will approve. I thought you and I weren't supposed to . . . you know, communicate much."

"Before, yeah. Mom and I had a really, really big fight about it right after Thanksgiving. I won. Like I totally won. I told her that I wanted to surprise you. Someday.

"Today is 'someday.'" Zadie declared.

So it was. I wasn't sure what to believe, so I asked:. "Mom's okay with you being here? I mean staying here with me?"

"I said if she said no, well tant pis. I'm outta there. I'd drop out of school. Earl even supported me!"

She slipped into Earl-speak, "You're a young, influenceable woman. Or-ee-gone's a sight better than France."

Maybe Earl wasn't as bad as I thought.

Was it important, I asked myself, to press Zadie for the truth? If not tonight, then when? Zadie was shaping her story like I had shaped mine. What was clear to me was that Zadie didn't need the third-degree or my uniformed advice; she needed to be loved and supported.

"Unless you don't want me here—"

"No, of course not! I would—absolutely, totally, more than anything in the world—love you to stay!" Making the unequivocal commitment made me feel good, like I had a purpose, a purpose that maybe I'd ignored for the last fifty or so years.

I rose, got a shovelful of wood pellets, and watched the flames respond as I dumped the pellets on the fire. The burning steadied, as did my resolve to make this situation work. I turned on a couple of lights, old school hurricane lamps but electrified and with pull-chains, and put a pot of water on the stove for pasta. The pot was one of those heavy, Costco, Kirkland pots made someplace not in China, I think Italy. The curved handle was difficult to grip with a potholder.

"Pasta and crab? Local crab. It's good. And I can thaw out a soup. Sorrel okay? It's foraged."

Zadie's voice lowered, not Earl-lower, but natural Zadie-lower. "I have conditions."

"About the soup?" I said with a nervous levity.

Loneliness was peaking at me from around the corner and screaming say yes, say yes to everything. "Whatever, I agree."

"This is a promise." Zadie paused to think—or so it seemed. She put her fingertips together and looked at the white paneled ceiling. "No, two promises! Wait, three!"

"Je le jure. Les trois."

"First, we speak French—only French, and for real. And, the second thing is you have to tell me the truth about how you learned French!"

"Oui et oui!"

I regretted agreeing to the latter as I uttered the second "oui."

"The third?" I asked.

"I don't want to talk too much about other stuff. I know you mean well."

I not only got it, I was relieved. "I'll try, but please don't give up on me if I slip."

I got a wink and a nod.

I still had the floor. "One condition." I was determined to step up to grandpa-hood. "We work this out with your mom and keep the B.S. to a minimum. Kali left a message on my phone. She's worried about you."

"Did you listen to it?" Zadie knew my habits.

"Yup, intro to outro."

"Rrr-right." The charade was over but she was undeterred. "I'm not going back, Papa Otto."

"Look, I'll stick up for you. But please talk to Mom. You don't want to fuck up like I fucked up."

We stared at each other, like we were waiting for the violins to break in or a commercial.

"Sorry. That was dumb." I tried to undo the damage. "Our situations are very different."

"I agree," she said, and extended her hand. "I agree with all of it. Fucked up, dumb, different."

We shook hands and laughed. Again, my hand was cold, hers warm. "You're funny, Pappa Otto."

"One little thing," I said. "Some of this histoire is—"

"I understand. Papa Otto, we're not going to kill a whole bottle of whiskey, just a sip." She raised her glass, squinted at it and *pointed to what would be a modest level of whiskey.* "This much. You decide. But no bullshit either. Okay?"

I nodded and smiled. "Like single malt, Zades, unblended. Starting when? I mean talking—"

"*Tout de suite!* [Right Now!]"

"*D'accord.* [Okay]" *I retrieved a half-full bottle of Pouilly-Fumé from the bottom of the fridge. Distracted by my thoughts, I bumped my head on the freezer handle as I stood up. I put the wine on the counter and made a second sortie, returning this time with crab, red Fresno peppers, parsley and frozen soup. Zadie found a cutting board and knife, and took the parsley from me. She looked around for the best place to work and selected the table. Nothing in my place was precious. The checkered tablecloth was stained from use.*

"*Alors, pose-moi tes questions!* [Well, ask away!]"

Her first question floored me: "*Tu as fusillé cet homme? En Iowa? C'est ce que j'ai extendu. Tu es allé en prison?* [Did you shoot that man? In Iowa. That's what I heard. Did you go to prison?]"

Shit! Elaine must have said something to Kali, or spoken directly to Zadie. Christ! I tossed down the last of my whiskey and stared at the fire. It was a lifetime ago, when I had shot at Jock, the lover-lumberjack. I remembered how dark it had been and that he hadn't groaned. Carol and I had skedaddled. The storm that clobbered us had flooded Mono lake. More to the point, no one ever showed up at the front door to arrest me. That said, I was no stranger to prison. In Zadie's mind, the two experiences were conflated.

"*Tu sais plus que je pensais. Laisse-moi essayer de te l'expliquer. Je garde ces trucs au fond de moi depuis longtemps. Ce n'est pas facile d'en parler.* [You know more than I thought. Let me try to explain. I've kept this stuff inside for a long time. It's not easy to talk about it.]" *As I said these words, that is, as I said them in French, I sensed the freedom derived from that peculiar quality of the*

French language that gives one permission to speak in the abstract about oneself and to say things that in English would feel awkward or uncomfortable.

"Absolument, je ne suis pas un meurtrier! Ce type qui nous avait attaqués avait un fusil de chasse. J'ai fait ce que je devais faire . . . [Absolutely, I'm not a murderer! This guy who attacked us had a shotgun. I did what I had to . . .]"

I relayed what had happened, sticking with my no B.S. promise and but omitting the details about the sex. Zadie didn't seem shocked. It was her way, to take things in and think about them. She challenged the account's credibility on one point.

"Une tempête tout à fait convenable, tu dirais pas? [Awfully convenient storm, wouldn't you say?]"

"Je te le jure, le corps a été englouti par une inondation et expulsé par une autre quelques ans plus tard. [I swear to god, the body had been swallowed up by one flood and spit out by another years later.]"

"Alors, ils on fait une analyse forensique? [Like, did they do a forensic analysis?]"

"Mon Dieu, Zades, je n'allais pas leur demander! [My god, Zades, I wasn't about to ask!]"

"Ouais, je comprends. Ne le fais pas, s''il te plaît! [Yeah, I get that. Please don't!]"

Zadie seemed satisfied. She pressed on, interested in Carol's fate and, I was hoping, little else.

"Et qu'est-ce qui est arrivé à ton amie, celle qui était enceinte? [And what happened to your friend, the one who was pregnant?]"

"*Quant à Carol, elle s'appelait Carole maintenant, elle est à Paris. Remariée, elle vit la vie d'une expat heureuse et enseigne à l'université. J'entends de ses nouvelles de temps en temps, seulement des messages courts.* [As for Carol—she spells it Carole now—she's in Paris. Remarried, living the life of a happy ex-pat and teaching at university. I hear from her now and then, only short notes.]"

"*Et le bébé? Est-ce qu'elle a eu l'enfant?* [The baby? Did she have the baby?]"

"*Mon filleul, si tu peux le croire, est aussi devenu enseignant.* [My godson, believe it or not, also became a teacher.]"

"*Ça me semble tellement normal et bizarre à la fois. Qu'est-ce . . .* [It all sounds so normal and weird at the same time. What —]"

"*Demain,* [Tomorrow,]" *I cut Zadie off,* "*garde tes questions pour demain. Préparons le dîner, mettons-nous d'accord avec Kali, et puis, j'ai une surprise!* [hold your questions for tomorrow. Let's make dinner, sort things out with Kali, and then I have a surprise!]"

"*Quelle surprise? Dis-le-moi!* [What surprise? Tell me!]"

It was time to lighten up. "*Je vais essayer de t'enseigner le 'Monster Mash'!* [I shall attempt to teach you the Monster Mash!]"

"*Pas possible!* [No way!]"

Zadie laughed and turned her head to the side, flashing an I'm-on-the-fence smile. She picked up a knife and started chopping parsley.

Tomorrow, she would be fresh. We can start studies for real. But what to read? So many brilliant French writers and thinkers! Why not Antoine de Saint-Exupéry!

I put the soup in the microwave to thaw and then filled a pot with water and put it on the stove. The burner clicked before igniting.

Life-changing choices were being made. Was there a role in Zadie's life for French language and culture?

I took a seat at the table and added whisky to my glass. "Déracinée. [Uprooted.]"

"*Qu'est-ce que ça signifie en anglais?* [What does that mean in English?]" *Zadie asked.*

 "*Uprooted. Casimir Pulaski a refait sa vie quand il a déménagé au nouveau monde et adopté une nouvelle langue.* [Casimir Pulaski had recast his life when he had moved to the new world and adopted a new language.]"

Zadie made the connection. "Ah, oui. Tu penses que je pourrais faire un bon 'Casi'? [Ah, yes. Do you think I could be a good 'Casi'?]"

"*Ben oui.* [Sure.]" *I decided to test the name:* "Casi, tu as faim? [Casi, are you hungry?]"

That went okay, not forced or awkward.

She listened and moved as if she were in front of a mirror and trying on a new hat. I visualized the name "Casi" dancing in her head.

"*Dis-le de nouveau.* [Say it again.]"

"Casi," *I said. This time I gave it a French lilt.*

"*Je l'aime bien. Et oui, je suis crevée!* [I like it. And yes, I'm starved!]"

She poked and shuffled parsley around on the cutting board, turning the knife this way and that, examining the fineness of what she had cut, and corralling sprigs that she had missed.

"*Papa Otto . . .*"

"*Oui?*"

There was a lively spurt of parsley chopping, then Casi stopped and looked up and right into my eyes. She smiled. "Je suis heureux. [I'm happy.]"

"*Tu voulais dire 'heureux' avec un 'x'?* [You intended 'happy' with an 'x'?]"

"*On verra. Mais . . . Oui.* [We'll see. But . . . Yes.]"

Author Bio

Wayne and his wonderful wife share a modest home a block from the beach in Manzanita, Oregon. He writes, climbs, and skis. His background includes long stretches of work in venture capital and project finance, and equally long stretches of study in philosophy, ancient Greek, and mathematics. He enjoys reading Shakespeare before bed, dancing salsa, cooking, and playing congas. He dearly wishes he knew a dozen languages but struggles mightily with the few with which he is familiar.

Learn more at wwgoss.com.